RACHEL LEIGH

"*Even in the bruised, deep dark,*
hope creates a tiny spark."
—Angie Weiland-Crosby

ZED

N othing.
      Silence.
Finally.
They've stopped.
The voices, the screams, the horror inside my head. Could it all be over?
Warm hands wrap around my arms and I swat them away. Only, they're not real. It's not over.
It will never be over.
That sick man still lives inside my head—touching my body and stealing my thoughts.
I have no choice. I have to do this.
My toes teeter on the edge of the cliff. My eyes close. Tilting my head back, I take in a deep, ragged breath right before I lean forward, ready to fall. Ready to escape the nightmare that never ends.
Almost there.
It's almost over.
My body drops, but I don't fall forward. My eyes open as my back hits the ground. "What the fuck!" I hiss. I push myself up

and bend my legs. Twisting around to get a look at the person who has a death wish. My chin drops to my chest when I see her. Releasing a pent-up breath, I huff, "What the hell are you doing here?"

"I need your help, Zed. They're coming for me."

I shake my head, turning it rapidly before I scream, "No! I'm done helping you." I point a finger behind her. "Now get the hell out of here or I'll take you over that cliff with me."

Her head shakes while her voice remains tranquil. "Oh no you don't. If I don't get to quit, neither do you."

"Go!" I scream even louder. My wrists go weak. My arms drop into the dirty sand, taking my body with them. I'm lying there curled up in the fetal position while she stands over me, holding witness to my demise. I can't do this anymore. I just can't.

Her arm sweeps under my head, hoisting it up. Her face hovering over mine. "If I have to live in this hell and burn because of my sins, so do you. Now suck it up. Pull yourself together and get your ass off this ground."

My eyes close, darkness drowning out her face. "You should have just let me jump."

"I won't let you do it. And if you try, I'll hold your hand and fly with you. Because if anyone deserves an easy out, it's me."

Looking up at her, while she cradles my head, I search for something. I'm not sure what it is about her, but she offered me a brief moment of calm and I want more of it. "Why are you here? I told you to never come near me again."

"I followed you to Rubble Edge. And now I'm staying with you, whether you like it or not."

Crawling onto my knees, I force myself off the ground and to my feet. "You ruined everything, you know that, right?"

"It's called survival. Are you ready to take your life back, Zed? Or do you plan on letting the monsters in your head win?"

I smirk. "You want me to live in this hell? Well, prepare yourself, Little Lamb, because nothing is more terrifying than a man who has no will to live."

Her arms cross over her chest as she tries to act all tough. "I'm not scared of you, Zed."

"That would be your second mistake. Your first was not letting me jump."

She'll soon learn that every choice has a consequence. If I'm being forced to face mine, it's time she faces hers, too.

CHAPTER ONE

ZED

You learn at a young age that when faced with a bear, you stand your ground—be tall, appear fearless. What they never told you, is that the strength you are forced to exhibit is all for show. You are not strong, you are not fearless, and most of all, you *cannot* dominate something with enough power to destroy you in two seconds flat.

All my life I've lived with the idea that if I appear big, bad, and ugly, the monsters can't touch me. I am fierce. I am tall. I am fearless. At least, that's what the world saw.

Until I lost my fight.

Until the moment when something in me snapped and I could barely muster the energy to crawl out of bed to face another day.

I am little. I am weak. And fear—fear has taken over. My soul is empty. The tick of my heart is only there because I haven't let it stop. Because I. HAVEN'T. LET. IT. STOP! The only thing I have any control over is that—whether I live, or die.

I hate that I was given such a gift. The gift of life. The choice to return it. Who would dare give me that power? Why can't the one who created me just make it for me? Take me out and end this madness once and for all.

Yet, here I am. A worthless bag of bones lying on the cold, hard floor of the bathroom because some foolish chick showed up at the wrong time and tried to save me. 'Tried' being the operative word. Just because I'm still here doesn't mean I've been saved.

Knock. Knock. Knock.

"Zed, if you don't open this damn door right now I'll break it down. I swear to ya, I will."

Knock. Knock. Knock.

Who the fuck does she think she is, anyway? I've helped her once, maybe twice, in my entire life and she thinks that she can just waltz into my personal hell and try to play the hero, because what, I deserve her help?

No. I don't deserve a damn thing. I'm owed nothing and I want nothing.

"Go away!" I screech. It was meant to sound demanding and harsh, but it comes out as a scratchy croak because the ability to even lift my head off this floor is futile.

My mind and my body are finally working together. Would have been nice if they did that years ago. When Mom was stuffing her face with pills and my mind said to stop her, but my hands wouldn't allow me to slap the bottle away. When that monster was touching me and I internally cried, but the tears failed to fall from my face. Or, when I was lying there with Marni and I knew I shouldn't touch her, but my fingers crept inside of her and dug deep, until they made her come around them.

Karma is a motherfucking bitch. And she's still pounding on the damn door.

"That's it. I'm coming in." There's a brief pause before the sound of her body crashing into the door echoes through the bathroom, rattling the picture on the wall that reads 'Hello Sweet Cheeks.' Another thud, and another, until the door swings open.

Motionless, I just lie there on my back, staring at the skylight in the ceiling. The sun is beginning to set and the fire-orange glow illuminates the tempered glass.

"That's it. Get the hell up." Vi grabs me by the arm and uses all of her strength to try and lift me off the floor, but it's not enough. She's one hundred pounds of flesh and bone with the brawn of a ten-year-old boy. But, she doesn't give up. Just like the Vi I remember—stubborn as an ox with the mouth of a sailor. Packs a good right hook, too.

My brows dip low in a scowl meant to show that her presence is not wanted. "Why the hell are you here?"

"Someone needs to be. You're wasting away, Zed."

"I'm fine!" I spit, pushing myself up into a sitting position. My bare arms hit the ceramic bathtub, cooling my sweltering skin.

I try to collect a thought or two, but the thing about not giving a fuck—you don't even care enough to think.

"We can help each other. Just like before. We're a good team."

Looking her dead in the eye, I drink up her vulnerability. She still wants my help. Everyone always wants my fucking help. "Haven't you realized by now that I'm not a team player?"

Sweeping her long black hair to one side, she slides over beside me. Her legs bend and she hugs her knees to her chest. "I think I'm the only one in the world who knows that, deep down, you are. You can pretend like you're a selfish asshole all you want, but I see beyond it, even if you can't feel it right now."

Snarling, I side-eye my unwanted guest. "I didn't ask for a therapist, so I suggest you drag your ass back to wherever you came from before I show you just how charred my heart has become."

"You've made it clear you don't want me here, but I'm staying. Wanna know why?"

"No," I quip.

"Because no one else is coming. No one cares about us, Zed. I told my parents adios and they just let me leave. Haven't heard from them since. You've been here for over a month and I can guess how many visitors you've had—none."

She isn't lying. What she doesn't realize is that I don't want visitors. Not her, not anyone. "Alright," I grab her arm and pull us both to our feet, "out you go." As I pull her toward the open door, she puts up a resistance by jerking her arm back and trying to get on the opposite side of me, away from the door. This girl has been a pain in my ass since I was a kid, and she's living proof that some things never change.

In an abrupt motion, I rotate her back around and push her arm against the wall. Her wrist is pinned over her head and her sea green eyes are wide with surprise. I tuck my chin, looking down at her. "You've got balls, baby girl." She's a petite little thing. I've got a good seven inches on her and I'm not talking about my cock that's growing into her thigh. She's probably five-foot-three, but she's got a loud mouth and tits that are slightly bigger than most girls with her frame. Her cleavage peeks out of the ripped v of her black Thrasher tee and for the first time in a while, something twinges inside of me. Whatever the feeling is, it offers me hope that I'm not completely dead inside—or maybe it's disappointment because it proves that I am, in fact, still alive.

Doe eyes dawn on me. Glossed over, full of lust and desire. Craving things I could never give her. Things I made clear that I wasn't capable of offering.

"It'll do you good to remember that. I don't shake under anyone's touch. Don't you know this by now?"

"The scar on the top of my head that feels like a wad of chewed gum is an ugly reminder. But you should also know that I'm not the same guy I was when you hit me over the head with that bottle two years ago." Grazing the pad of my thumb under her chin, I tip her head up. "I've changed."

"Everyone does."

Trailing my fingers steadily over her bottom lip, I watch. *I wonder if she still tastes the same as she did back then?* Like Friday night sin and Sunday morning breakfast. I could devour her now and find out, but then she'd never leave. "Go back to school, Vienna."

"I quit school. Haven't been there in almost a month."

Stupid girl. Though, she's not stupid, quitting school was the dumbest fucking thing she could do. Vi is smart and she's got a bright future ahead of her if she just lets go of all this shit. She's classy in her own emo way. She values things like PETA and the right to carry. She'd kill a human for a meal before she would an animal. It's deranged how true that statement is.

"Why the fuck would you do that?"

She takes a step back and hangs her head down as she scrunches her toes in her black flip flops. "I don't fit in there. I don't fit in anywhere."

"Welcome to my fucking world. But don't get too comfortable in it, because your ass is outta here first thing in the morning." I dip out the door into the hall, shaking my head in agitation.

I came here to get away from people. Not just some, but all of them. Haven't turned my phone on in three days and really didn't think I ever would again. I went to Rubble Edge with no intention of ever coming back. I was ready to make my escape. Leave this dreaded bullshit life behind. Then she showed up and threw a wrench in my plans.

She might be tough, but everyone has a breaking point. It's about time that I find hers.

CHAPTER TWO

F lipping on the water, I press my palms to the cold marble counter and watch it create a little tornado effect before swirling down the drain.

I knew coming here was a risk. I'm probably the last person Zed wants to see. Our entire lives we just pretended the other didn't exist, as far as everyone was concerned. Then one fateful night, I stopped pretending.

I can't go back to Redwood. Ever. I mean, how could I? They're onto me. They know what I did.

Regret is a pesky little thing. It eats away at your insides while you're forced to hold it together on the outside. For months, I was able to do just that. I played the dutiful sister who lost her brother—I walked the line, shed the tears.

It was all for show. Sure, I regret the way things went down. But, I don't regret what I did. My brother was a monster. Not the kind that hides under your bed. No, he was the kind that wore his crazy proudly. He didn't need to hide, because he had control over everyone inside that house.

The memories of my past creep up from time to time and hit me like a hurricane.

"*Vi, he's almost here,*" Mom hollers from the bottom of the stairwell.

"*Don't care,*" I sputter in a hushed tone as I sit on the bench of my vanity. With a bent leg and my foot propped in front of me, I stroke another layer of black polish on my toenails.

"*Vi!*" Mom shouts even louder in her authoritative pitch that is meant to be intimidating. "*Get down here, now!*"

"*Ugh. Fine.*" I raise my voice and scream at the top of my lungs, "*I'm coming!*" I drop the brush back in the jar of polish and screw the top on.

I don't know why my mother thinks that it's necessary to drag in every Tom, Dick, and Harry who needs a home, but here comes another. Apparently his name is Luca and he's some troubled boy who needs a place to crash while finishing his senior year.

Walking with my wet toes spread, I watch them, making sure they don't smear.

"*Vi!*" she hollers, yet again.

"*I'm coming!*" I glare at her from the top of the stairs. Mom stands looking prim and proper, as usual. Her honey blonde hair in a tight bun, not a strand out of place. A three-piece navy suit, ironed to perfection, and closed-toed heels to match.

She waves her hand rapidly, calling me down. "*Hurry, he just pulled up.*" She gives me a double take, and I know what's coming—a critique of my appearance. "*Would it have hurt you to put on something more presentable? And what in God's name is that on your toes? Pink, Vienna. Girls wear pink.*"

Ignoring her, like I always do, I walk past her and throw myself down on her all-white sofa, curling my legs underneath me like a pretzel.

Oops.

I lift my leg and look down, realizing I just smeared OPI Midnight Black all over her Plume Blanche sofa. I only know the name because for a month straight no one was allowed to sit on it. Before she'd leave the house, she'd always tell us, '*don't sit on my new Plume Blanche Sofa.*'

Well, I sat and I smeared.

Mom waves her hands again, like she's airing away a nasty fart, as she tries to call me to her side. My highbrow family is all lined up horizontally at the door, waiting like soldiers, ready to welcome this poor boy into our lives.

I shake my head. "Nope."

"Vienna Moran, you get your behind up here right now."

If I stand, she will lose her ever-loving mind once she sees what lies beneath me. "I've got cramps. Think I started my period."

In two seconds flat, she's at my side. "On my Plume Blanche sofa?" She takes hold of my arm and yanks me up.

I wince, looking back and forth from her to the crow shit streaks I left behind.

"Ahhh," she gasps. "My Plume Blanche sofa."

If I hear her say those words one more time, I might vomit all over the polish stain and then we'll have bigger problems.

"It's fine, Mom. I'll take some remover to it—"

Before I can finish, the doorbell rings. Mom still stands there in astonishment and pays no attention as the door opens and the temporary member of our family walks in.

I notice, though.

Tall, muscular, tan, with a grunge appeal.

He's perfect.

A smack on the door snaps me out of my daydream. Zed stands at the doorway with his hand against the frame. "Are you about done sulking in here because I was planning to take a shower?"

I look down and notice the water is still running, so I put my hands under the running stream. "Uh, yeah, I was just washing my hands." I give them a shake then push the handle down, shutting the water off.

As soon as I turn around, I slam right into a wall of abs. I'm not sure when he rid himself of his shirt, but I'm certainly not complaining—in fact, I catch myself staring. It seems that solitude has been good for him. He might not be clean-shaven, and he's in dire need of a haircut, but he's more defined than I've ever seen him.

"Well?" he says, or asks. I'm not really sure.

My eyes skate up from the smooth skin of his chest, stopping at the sleeve of tattoos on his left arm. Blue and purple corded veins bulge to the surface of his skin. Looking all the way up, I find his chiseled jaw and soft, pouty lips. "Yeah, sorry." I go to walk around him and for the first time in a very long time, I see the corner of his lip tug up in an egotistical grin.

He reaches out, collaring me by my forearm. In a swift pull, my body crashes into his. Slow steps walk us backward until my back hits the far wall of the room.

"What are you doing?" I choke out in an audible breath.

Careless fingers creep up the side of my shirt as his Adam's apple bobs in his throat. Stone-colored eyes stare back at me and for the first time ever, I feel powerless under Zed's gaze. "Isn't this what you want? Isn't this why you're here?" His breath hits the nape of my neck, sending chills down my back.

His fingers nestle on my side under the strap of my bra. My nipples harden against the fabric, back tensing, hands trembling. "No, I came because I was worried about you."

"Liar!" he shouts, alarming every cell in my body.

"Zed, I don't—"

"Shhh," he whispers, pressing a finger to my lips. He proceeds to run the tip of his finger around my mouth.

I go to speak, which was the wrong move, because he uses the opportunity to slide his finger inside my mouth. On impulse, I bite down. A metallic taste seeps onto my tongue.

"Fuck!" He pulls his finger out and while he examines the bite marks, I feel pretty damn pleased with myself. "Wrong move, Little Lamb." He pushes me back against the wall. With his body cloaking mine, he takes me by the wrist and pins my hand over my head.

With his free hand, he grabs the collar of my V-neck shirt and pulls so hard that the fabric splits down past my breasts.

My head tilts to the side as his lips skim my collarbone. "I didn't come here for this."

He doesn't lift his head when he speaks, just keeps exploring me like I'm his own personal plaything. "Then why aren't you stopping me?"

I should. I could shove him back right now and throw a couple punches to his face. Wouldn't be the first time. In fact, the freak in him would probably enjoy it.

For some reason, I don't stop him. Even if I don't want this. I'm too curious to see how far he will take it. Will his hand slide down farther? Will it tremble when it does?

As if he reads my mind, his nails scratch against my stomach as he rims the waistband of my jean shorts. With one hand, he pops the button. His head lifts, eyes locked back on mine. It's his way of searching for approval, which I won't give him, because even if I did fight him off, he'd dominate me. Zed takes what he wants and shows no mercy.

I hate that I'm so turned on by that fact.

Still watching me, his hand slithers down the opening of my shorts. I'm slightly embarrassed by the fact that he's going to find dampened panties and he'll immediately know that I'm more into this than I'm letting on.

"Want me to stop?" he asks, before going further.

"Does it matter?"

His lip snarls in a pompous smirk. Nostrils flared, and eyes wide like saucers. "No," he says. At least he's truthful in that aspect. "Tell me something, Vi. How old are you now?"

"Turned eighteen yesterday," I quip with sarcasm.

"Very nice," he retorts in a smooth manner.

Before I can even question his blatant response, his fingers lunge inside of me so fast that my entire body jolts upward, my feet almost leaving the ground. I gasp at the temporary pain. One, two, three fingers buried deeply. "You're wet, Vi," he tsks, "seems you didn't want me to stop, after all."

Instead of sliding his fingers in and out of me, he just pulsates the tips. Drumming against my walls. I feel the scrape of his fingernail, and it's not pleasurable at all. "Zed," I say in a muffled groan.

Ignoring me, he grabs one of my legs and props it at his side. "Zed," I say again. Feeling tears well in my eyes. "Stop."

He doesn't listen; he just keeps going, and I try to force myself to fall into the rhythm, so I can enjoy it.

"What's that?" he finally responds, as his hard cock grinds against my pelvic bone. His fingers drive farther and harder, causing me to clench my thighs around his hand.

"That hurts."

"Come on, Vi. You're a tough girl. Either take what I'm giving to you, or fight back." He begins twisting his hand as his fingers dig deeper inside of me, as if he's searching for something.

Is he testing me?

In one swift motion, I bring my head forward, knocking it against his. There's a dull pain that signals the start of an awful headache. Probably hurt me more than him, but it grabs his attention. His fingers stop moving. "There's the Vi I remember." He smirks in delight.

I grab his arm and pull it out of my shorts. Then, I plant my hands to his chest and shove him backward while he laughs in devilish hysterics.

"You're right. I am tough." I shove him again until his back is against the door and it latches shut. "Next time you want something from me, ask." I grit through my teeth, right in front of his face.

The next thing I know, his mouth is crashing into mine, giving me all he's got while I return the favor. Our tongues twist and tangle, our lips smacking and sucking. This kiss is so deep, hard, and forced that my mind enters a state of complete euphoria. I have no control over my own body as my hands rid him of his pants, and my own clothing. Until we're standing there, two naked, broken souls, ready to devour one another.

I freeze. He does the same. We stare at each other, questioning what happens next. I'm not sure if I've even grasped that this is happening.

Then we're at it again. Zed eats up the space between us and slams his body into mine, hoisting me up until my back crashes into the wall so hard that I fear my tailbone has shattered. His hands cup my ass while my legs wrap around him, ankles locked and toes curled. He doesn't even hesitate before shoving his cock inside of me.

My mouth's agape, fingers clenching his shoulders and my breasts pulverized against his chest.

"Now, tell me you want me to stop." He breathes out in a heady exhale, his voice barely even recognizable.

I cry out, "Don't you dare." His pelvic bone crashes into me while my ass slides up and down, bouncing on his cock.

My head falls back, mouth dropped open. "Oh my God," I whimper. He's bigger than I remember, and he completely fills me up, to the point that I can feel the head of his cock bob inside my stomach.

His eyes squint and he releases a coarse grunt as he pounds into me. Eyes cement to mine, and fingertips dig into the bone of my ribs on either side of my waist.

I hold on tightly to his neck when he moves his hands to the wall. His teeth graze the corner of his lips before he presses them back to mine. My lip ring pulls between his teeth, stretching it to the max, but I relish the pleasure it brings me.

With my hands still wrapped around his neck, my fingertips pierce his skin as I slide them down and cry out in pleasure. "Zed!"

"Fuck, Vi..." His words trail off as I feel his head swell and pulsate inside of me. I continue to ride out his rhythmic movements. His breaths become labored and unfulfilled. Mine, nonexistent. I clench around him, my entire body shooting with tingles as we both combust at the exact same time.

My feet hit the floor and he slides out, our arousal dripping down my legs and onto the marbled floor.

Zed grabs a towel and tosses it at me, hitting me in the face. "Thanks," I scoff.

"Hurry up. I need a shower," he says sternly before he walks out the door stark naked.

Once the door is closed behind him, my shoulders drop. I'm not sure how I feel about what just happened.

The only feeling Zed has shown me in a significant amount of time is loathing, and maybe a smidgeon of gratitude, but mostly loathing.

It's no secret to either of us that he once made my stomach flip-flop and my heart race, but that was years ago.

That was before our worlds fell apart.

CHAPTER THREE

ZED

An hour later, Vi comes out and I take her place in the bathroom. She doesn't even look at me as she passes by. My clothes drop to the floor and I step into the scalding-hot shower; I revel in the burn against my bare skin. Each drop of water that pricks every follicle on my body brings me one step closer to reprieve.

When you start to feel like you're losing your mind, you do just about anything to feel normal. I still feel pain, hunger, desire. My body still works. My thoughts are still there. Even the ones that I wish would die off.

Vi's unwanted arrival shook up my plans a bit, but maybe it's true that everything happens for a reason. Maybe I'm not finished yet for a reason.

Fuck that. It's not true.

If that were the case, there would be reasons for all the bad shit that happens. In my case, I am that reason. I've brought every fucking thing on myself and really can't blame anyone aside from that dirty, rotten pastor and my father.

But it's because of all those vile acts that she's here right now. Trying to save me or whatever she thinks she's doing. Personally,

I think she's just scared shitless and has nowhere to run. I'm not sure why she always thinks I'm her safety net, but I wish she'd just forget about all the times I've helped her in the past and stay away like I told her to.

As much as I hate to admit it, Vi is like the female version of me. She's a loner, she's deep, and she's done things that would surprise the devil himself.

I guess when you're raised in fucked-up way, you become fucked-up.

Something about her has changed, though. Not only the fact that she now fills out her bra and her ass is as round as a pair of basketballs. But she's finally comfortable in her own skin. For so long, she was told how she was supposed to act and it wasn't until Josh died that she became the person she wanted to be.

Why am I even thinking about this? I don't give a damn about this girl.

She can be a fucking gnat on the wall or a queen on a throne and I could still care less.

"Whatcha looking at?" Mom asks from beside me as I stand at the kitchen window. Her bones frail and her hair as coarse as hay.

"Nothing, Ma." I peel my eyes away and look over at her, my expression shifting from curious as to what Vi's doing, to concerned with my mom's health. "You feeling okay today?"

A strangled smile raises her cheekbones. "Better than yesterday. I think today will be a good day." She pulls me in for a hug and I allow her arms to envelop me for the first time in a while. "She's a beautiful girl, Zed."

My head descends so I can get a better look at Mom's expression. "Who?"

Boney knuckles graze the top of my head. "You know who. Vienna. Reminds me a lot of you. Quiet and stubborn to a fault."

"And a pain in the ass?"

"Watch your mouth." She teases a smack to my shoulder. "Girls like that are a rarity, son. If they keep their mouth shut when they have

nothing to say, but scream loud when they want to be heard, they're keepers. The world is full of followers. That girl over there is a leader."

A low rumble climbs up my throat. "You barely even know her."

"I know enough. You and I are a lot alike, Zed. We prefer to stand back and observe. That's how we find out who people really are." She walks back over to the window and presses her palms to the edge of the kitchen sink. "Look at her just lying there in that grass without a care in the world. An entire bus of high school students could come back and it wouldn't faze her one bit."

Mom's right. Vi is something special. Her hands lay against either side of her as her fingers pull at the grass. Pick, pull, toss. Pick, pull, toss. She stares straight at the sun with her eyes wide open, as if the light could never be too bright. She's different, but she's my kind of different.

I grab a bottle of body wash and squirt it into my hand, then lather it up, rubbing it all over, from head to toe, getting every crack and crevice. When I stroke my cock, her face pops into my head. The expression she wore while I was fucking her.

I pump myself a few times, hoping that it won't disappoint me this time like it has in the past when I jerk off. It's been awhile since I've even been able to get an erection and even when I do, I just can't focus enough to get off. Vi woke something inside of me and I need to be sure it wasn't a fluke. I always just assumed it was my punishment for my sins. It wasn't until I found her in the bathroom all doe-eyed and nervous that I was reminded of just how much my body reacts to her.

My cock begins to harden in my hand as my body begins to fill up with that insatiable need for release again. Jolts of electricity shooting through every cell inside of me. My head drops back, letting the hot water fall on my face. I pump harder and faster, that last encounter still etched in my memory like a fresh painting. Her perky breasts, her tight pussy. Emerald eyes full of wonder staring back at me as my dick plunged inside of her.

Vi might be a handful, but she's my kind of sexy.

With one hand on the wall of the shower, I stoop down and continue to stroke until my cum shoots all over the bathtub. I pump a few more times, then run my hand under the water and grab some more soap to finish cleaning up—feeling really fucking proud of myself. And pretty pleased that my dick is working again.

It's been awhile since I felt any ounce of hope, and while my life might still be in shambles, it's sort of nice to know I've got company for the ride. Misery loves company, or however that bullshit goes.

I kill the water and step out onto the drying mat on the floor. Water drips off of me and I realize that I never grabbed a fresh towel from the linen closet outside of the bathroom.

Pulling the door open, I step into the hall and walk three feet to the towels. Whoever built this house wasn't thinking about the possibility that one might want their bath towels in the bathroom.

As soon as I turn to go back, a five-foot-three ghoul girl comes scampering out from one of the bedrooms in a pair of grey booty shorts and a white crop top tee. I give her a once-over. Standing there, butt-ass naked, I watch her face flush red. "We've gotta quit meeting like this."

She hides her tinged cheeks with her hands, and it's a new look seeing Vi unsettled. "I was just..." she pivots left and right in front of me as I stand in the middle of the hall, "just going to make something to eat." She lifts her head up to stare at the ceiling, avoiding the alternative.

Being the gentleman that I am not, I just let the towel hang at my side and my cock that was hard, then semi-soft, is now hard again. And I'm on fucking cloud nine because he ain't letting me down today. Three times in the past hour—pretty sure that's a new record.

She doesn't even look at me as she slides past so I start walking, bypassing the bathroom and heading straight for my room.

Not sure why she's bothered so much. It was only an hour ago that she couldn't keep her hands off this body.

My clothes lay in a mound on the floor that resembles a black trash bag. Everything I own is black. I prefer one solid color and what better choice than the color of my heart?

I throw on a tee shirt—black—and a pair of joggers—also black. You won't be seeing me in those grey joggers that the ladies love. If I'm not in black, I'm naked.

Feeling mentally and physically exhausted, I drop my back on the bed and stare up at the ceiling. I've been in this house for over a month and it still doesn't feel like home to me. Granted, it's not my home. It's some luxurious Airbnb packed away in seclusion, east of Brayburn City. I could have chosen one of Dad's houses that are scattered all over the US, but I didn't want anyone to find me. Little good that did.

I'm still not even sure how Vi tracked me down. She said she followed me, but when? Jumping to my feet, I scurry down the hall to the kitchen. I can see she's making herself comfortable here. Coffee drips into the pot and she's bent over the counter, looking at her phone.

Her head lifts and she looks at me with no shame in making herself at home. "Making coffee, want some?"

"No. I don't *want some*. I wanna know how you found me here? Does anyone else know where you're at?"

When she starts playing some music from her phone and her shoulders sway to the beat, I snatch it away from her. "Hey," she huffs.

"How'd you find me, Vi?"

"I told you, I followed you. Now give me that." Her bony fingers try to grab the phone away, but I hold it over my head.

"When?"

She jumps up to grab it, but her short ass would need a chair, and even that's a stretch.

"A few days ago. I was following Wyatt McCoy because he's

been fishing for info with your crew and he ended up at Tommy's cabin. You were there, and I followed you." She says it so point-blankly, like she just followed me to a party or something.

"You followed me two hours to Brayburn and everywhere I went in between?" Shane's house, the airport, the cemetery. "Why?"

Giving up, she stops jumping and realizes that if she wants her phone back, she's giving me answers. "Because I'm nosey and I like to know what to expect from people. I got a room in the city, then yesterday when I came to make my presence known, you drove to that cliff. I stayed back for a bit, but once I realized what you were doing, I had no choice but to stop you."

My glare holds tight to her eyes. "You should have stayed away."

"You keep saying that, but here you are—alive." She swings around, her long black hair smacking my bare arm. "You're welcome."

My lungs deflate as the air blows out in a huff. "You expect me to thank you?"

"I saved your life." Her shoulders rise and she smiles with an extra few bats of her long lashes. This girl infuriates me to no end. Unlike any other human in this entire world ever has.

"You know they can trace you on this thing."

"It's on airplane mode. No one will find us."

"So you thought you'd just interfere like you always do." My arm lowers, but I still grip her phone tightly in the palm of my hand.

"It's a good thing, too, because no one else does and if it weren't for me, you'd be a goner—muerta, mort—"

"Okay, I get the fucking point. You can speak languages I don't understand."

"Dead," she continues, "you'd be fucking dead. So, once again, you're welcome." Casually, like we were just standing here talking about the weather, she grabs a mug and fills it to the brim with black lava, just like her soul—the one I plan to take.

"You've got until morning and then you're out of here, assuming you survive the night." I give her a wink.

She mumbles with sarcasm, "You'd really kick me out on the week of my birthday? Come on, Zed, have a heart."

"Goodnight, Vienna," I quip, before turning on my heel and going to my room to lie down with my eyes wide open until the sun rises.

That's how my nights go. I don't sleep; I just think.

CHAPTER FOUR

Warmth radiates my cold hand as I grip the mug tightly. I flinch when Zed's bedroom door closes. I hate that I'm so jumpy all the time. I sneeze and scare the shit out of myself. The only thing worse than living a life where you feel like you're constantly looking over your shoulder, is living a life where you *have* to.

For some reason, I've decided that seeking comfort in Zed was the best option. What the hell was I thinking? Maybe it's because he's the only person who has ever given me any real comfort. No one knows that, though. Everything about Zed and I has been this secret. He thought it would be best if we weren't associated with each other after everything that happened—before and after.

But that was years ago. It all feels like this distant memory, yet it still sits like a hundred-pound barbell in the forefront of my mind.

Gawking like a horny teen, I stand there observing while Mom hovers over the housekeeper, making sure she removes every bit of polish on the sofa.

Tall, dark, and handsome drops his bag on the floor at his feet. "Nice digs. So, where's this room I'm staying in?" He scopes out the place like a criminal eyeing the most prized possessions in sight.

"You'll be in the east wing with your own private access. However, there are a few rules we need to go over." Dad picks up Luca's bag and shoves it into his chest. "Touch my daughter and I'll kill you."

With that, Dad walks away, but Mom skedaddles to the new kid's side, treating him as though he's a toddler who just scraped his knee. "Pay no attention to Mr. Moran, he's a bit on the outspoken side." Mom takes Luca's bag and holds out an arm, gesturing for him to go first.

It makes me sick, really. Mom babies these orphans, yet snubs her nose at her own flesh and blood daughter.

Stopping in front of me, our guest tips his chin. "And you are?"

"Vi, your new sister. Welcome to hell." I waggle my brows before skipping out of the room and up the stairs.

Two minutes later, there's a knock at my door and before I can respond, it flies open. "Get your ass up and go tell them to make that fucking rat leave," Josh spits out in a fit of rage.

My heart drums in my chest because I didn't even know he was home; otherwise, I'd have locked the door.

I scooch to a sitting position, ready to take flight if necessary. "Do Mom and Dad know you're home?"

"Fuck if I care. Where the hell were you last night?" He walks over and begins shuffling through my nightstand drawer.

My back steels and my stomach twists into tiny tight knots. "I went to the library. I go to the library every Monday night."

The drawer slams shut and my body jolts. "Vienna," he tsks with a menacing look on his face. "Where is it?"

"I threw it away. Why keep a journal if someone else keeps taking it and reading it." I spring to my feet and head for the door, but I'm not fast enough. Josh strikes it with his hand and it latches closed. The lock clicks, alarming every fiber of my being. "Let me out or I'll scream. There's a new member of this household, and...and he's bigger than you. He can kick your ass."

"Oooh, I'm so scared." He shivers in full-blown mockery.

"You should be." I grab the handle again, but this time, Josh shoves me back so hard that I land on my ass and slide a foot across the hardwood floor.

"This is my fucking house. Keep that in mind, and I'll make damn sure our new brother knows the same."

It wasn't always like that. There was a time there was peace in the Moran family. Life was never normal, but at least the maniac didn't live here and control us all with an iron fist. Mom took him in because her conscience doesn't handle guilt well. Josh was a ward of the state his entire life until Mom saved him. In doing so, she destroyed the rest of us. Josh might be responsible for what happened to Luca, but Mom loaded the gun, figuratively speaking.

∞

"RISE AND SHINE," Zed singsongs, all too chipper for someone who was ready to die yesterday. "Time to get on the road and get you back out of my life." The curtains draw open, and the sun beams directly on my face.

I shriek like a vampire, pulling the pillow over my face. "Really, Zed. Is that necessary?"

"Sure is. Now get your ass up. Train leaves in ten minutes." He walks out, leaving me lying there, basking in the glow of the morning sunrise.

"But the sun just fucking rose," I blubber—to myself, because he's long gone out the door.

Seconds later, I hear the engine of his truck purr to life. *He really is kicking me out.*

Flinging the blanket off me with a few airy huffs, I smack my feet against the hardwood floors until I'm standing at the front door. Looking outside, it feels like I'm at a different house. Yesterday, a dark cloud descended on me and everything was hazy and dead. Today, the sun is out, the grass is green, and the birds are chirping at an empty feeder perched on a shepherd's hook.

I waltz over to the driver's side of the truck, my feet dampening from the dew on the grass. Pretty strange for the dry spell cast on the state all last month. Zed's window is all the way down and he doesn't even look at me as he releases a cloud of smoke from his lungs.

Sweeping it away, I press a hand to my hip. "You know, you're teasing those birds with the feeder hanging there. How would you like it if you were starving and I put an empty plate in front of you?"

His head twists, brow cocked. "You fucking serious right now?"

"Dead serious. It's not fair to them."

His mouth wraps around the butt of the cigarette, the cherry coming to life at the end. He draws in a drag, holds it, and speaks on the clipped exhale. "Listen, Dr. Doolittle, you've got thirty seconds to get your ass in the front seat of this truck or I'll personally toss you in myself. I'd choose the former, because I'm not gentle."

My arms cross over my chest. "No."

"Excuse me?"

"I said, no. I'll walk to my car if I have to, but I'm not getting in that truck."

"You'll walk three miles down a beaten terrain in the desert instead of catching a ride with me?"

"Mmhmm. Because once we get there and I get in my car, what will you do? Drive your truck over the ledge?"

"Look, girl. I know you think the world is all sunshine and rainbows—albeit your choice in clothing—but it's not. If I wanted to drive my truck over that ledge or even jump, why the fuck would I have woken you up? You really think that your nagging voice is the last thing I'd want to hear before dropping to my death?"

He's got a point.

"Fine. But, can I at least take a shower first? I'm still all sandy from dragging your ass off the ground yesterday."

His eyes close softly, his lashes fluttering while his jaw ticks. "Hurry your ass up."

I bite back a smile, until he tosses his lit cigarette out the window and it lands centimeters from my foot. "Really? You couldn't just snub that out and throw it in the trash?"

I bend over and pick it up, stretching my arm outward to keep from breathing in the smoke.

He smirks, and while it's not a full-blown smile, it's heaps and bounds to what I witnessed yesterday. "I'll tell you what, I'll let you take a shower *and* eat breakfast if you take a drag of that cigarette."

"Fuck no!" I spit. "I prefer to take care of my body, and the planet."

"Come on, birthday girl. Live a little."

"You're deranged and this is peer pressure at its worst. What would watching me take a hit off a cigarette satisfy?"

His shoulder rises. "Nothing. But, it'll be fun to watch."

"It would be for you. Relishing in the discomfort of others. Welcome back, Zed." I bring my arm closer, peering down at the lit butt in my hand. I've never smoked a cigarette before. In fact, I've never inhaled anything but fresh air, and maybe some bonfire smolders.

Giving him one last look, I notice him watching me intently. This sick fuck is probably getting turned on by this. Controlling bastard that he is. My lips part, and I wrap them around the nasty thing that literally tastes like ash. I breathe in—straight in, giving the smoke a direct shot to my lungs.

My mouth closes and I begin choking, but don't open my mouth as the air coughs up, bringing the smoke with it. When I can't take anymore, my lips part again and it all comes rolling out in a raspy bark.

Zed starts laughing, finding pleasure in my discomfort.

My hand claps over my mouth as I continue to clear my lungs. "That's so gross." His door opens and his black boots hit the paved driveway. I drop the still burning cigarette on the ground. "Step on that," I tell him.

His toe digs into it, extinguishing the cherry, then I bend down and pick it back up.

"I thought you changed," he says. "Seems you're still little Vi, who lets everyone tell her what to do." He pats a hand to my cheek like I'm a child. I swat it away, but he grabs me by the wrist, squeezing so tightly that my fingertips become pale and cold. He bites down, clenching his teeth. "Start standing up for yourself or the people in this fucked-up world will eat you alive." He gives my wrist a jerk as he drops it at my side.

I wanna say something, but I'm at a loss for words as I watch him walk back to the house. I know exactly who he's talking about. His friends are looking for me. For whatever reason, Zed hasn't tossed me out, yet.

I wanna trust him, but he's so compulsive. I wouldn't put it past him to hand me over to his friends just because he likes to be cruel. Should have known there was a reason behind his antics. Zed King doesn't do anything without purpose. Even with the cigarette, he knew I'd take a puff if he pushed me hard enough.

CHAPTER FIVE

ZED

S he's too easy.

You make a few small threats or offer a reward and people will do pretty much anything you want them to. I always thought Vi was different. There's no doubt that she's tough. But she's gone from obeying her mom and dressing the way she's told, to finally being herself—at least that's what I thought.

Swinging the cupboard open, I grab a loaf of bread, unsure how long it's been in there. Pretty sure I bought it last week. I pull out two slices, one being the heel end, and drop them in the slots of the toaster on the counter, then press the lever down.

One thing I am is a man of my word.

I might not do things the way people expect them to be done, but if I say I'll do it, I do. Sometimes half-assed, but other times, I put a great deal of time and effort into it. This time it's the latter.

Vi storms into the kitchen with puckered brows. "You played me."

"I didn't do anything. I fed you a line, you took the bait. And now I'm making you breakfast."

"I'm not weak, Zed."

"Never said you were."

"You implied it. For your information, the reason I don't want to leave has nothing to do with me and everything to do with you."

Her words grab my attention as I'm folding up the bread bag and stuffing it back in the cupboard. "What's that supposed to mean?"

There's an awkward beat of silence while she unscrambles the words in her head and I anticipate what she's going to say. "I don't want you to die, Zed."

Something qualms in my chest. I don't even know how to react to that statement. No one has ever said that to me before. I mean, people don't usually walk around telling others that they don't want them to die, but Vi is the only person who noticed I even wanted to. Tommy said he was gonna check on me, but I haven't given him the opportunity. I'm not even sure that anyone else would come if they knew I was on the verge of taking my life.

No one really cares. But for some reason, Vi does.

"Why?" I ask point-blankly as I pull open the drawer and grab a butter knife.

She spins around, giving me her back and making it really fucking awkward for both of us.

Neither of us are good with emotions and if she thinks she's gonna stand here and spill her heart, she's sadly mistaken. I won't allow it.

"We've lived the same life, Zed. Behind closed doors, you were the only friend I've ever had."

The toast pops up, but I ignore it. My hand flies out in front of me. "Stop right there, Vienna."

"Don't call me that!" She spins around, her expression full of disdain.

"Then don't dredge up shit in the past. Neither of us wanna relive that mess." I grab the two slices in one hand and drop them on a paper plate.

She comes closer, my body suddenly tensing up. I'm not sure if it's the slow and steady steps she's taking, or the way she's looking at me as though she's trying to read me. I take a step back. "What are you doing?" She takes another forward. Her hand comes toward me and I crane my neck to avoid her touch. "Stop it."

But she doesn't. Her hand rests on my cheek like that little girl in the vampire movie who tries to make you feel shit. "It might be a sordid past, but it's ours. It's our present, it's our future, it's our secret." I push her hand away, feeling uneasy at the moment she's trying to create. "Zed," the way she says my name makes me feel nauseous, "embrace it. And maybe, eventually, we can both heal from it."

"Get the fuck away from me," I deadpan. Scrunching my nose like she's sour milk in my cup.

Her eyes well with tears and I fucking hate it. "Why are you like this?" she asks, knowing the answer.

"You know why."

"Say it out loud."

"Fuck you."

"Say it, Zed."

"I said, fuck you!" I shout so loudly that the words echo through my own ears before they start ringing. My body feels like it's caught fire and my hands begin trembling.

Vi grabs ahold of me, holding my hands in hers. "He can't hurt us anymore."

She's wrong. He still hurts me. He still haunts me. He's in my thoughts; he's in my dreams. Doesn't he do the same to her?

"He can't touch us."

Her hands skate down my arms and without thought, I push her back with little force and turn to get away from this psychotherapist.

Is this my fucking punishment?

Her?

The girl who shakes my world up and never even blinks in the process. She screams humanity and purity, but digs her nails into my heart, just to try and make me feel something.

Well, hats off to her—she did it.

As I approach the door, I draw back a fist and release. My knuckles colliding with the drywall beside the doorframe and busting through, leaving a huge-ass hole in the wall. "Fuck!" I shout, shaking my hand, then pulling the door open and rushing out.

She makes me feel rage. An uncontrollable fury. The desire to run and never stop while I leave everything and everyone behind me.

Everyone but her.

I hate that she makes me feel. She's the only person in the entire world who can bring me to my knees and I fucking hate her for it.

I don't stop. My feet don't allow it. Bypassing my truck, I just keep going.

Down the open trail that turns into dry sand. I can see mountains in the distance. If only I could run to them and hide away. But, fuck that. This was supposed to be my hideaway. She shouldn't even be here.

"Zed, wait," she hollers. The smacking of her flip-flops rings closer and closer. I can hear her heavy breaths and when I sense her presence at my side, I get even more agitated.

"Go, Vi."

"I'm not leaving you."

I come to an abrupt stop and spin to face her. My hands grip her forearms as I walk her backward. "I'm not kidding. If you don't get the hell away from me right now, I will lose my mind. This is not a drill. This is not a fucking game. Go. Away." I'm really trying to be as gentle as I know how.

"You're a fucking coward," she spits, literally. Spraying her words all over my face.

"And you're a bitch," I spew on impulse. She's not really a bitch. She's actually very...

Her open palm slaps my face.

My body reacts before my mind and I raise my hand, but she grabs my arm. Wide eyes and dilated pupils glare back at me. "You were gonna hit me!"

"I was gonna fucking stop you."

"Liar. You raised your hand to hit me." Smack. She hits me again. Bringing the sting from the last blow to the surface. "I can't believe you almost hit me."

Clenching my teeth, I close my eyes and take a few steady breaths. My hand grazes over my burning cheek. "You fucking—"

Smack. Again. She's testing my limits. That's exactly what she's doing.

I will not snap.

"Are you done yet?"

"Are you?"

My hands fly to the side of my head, gripping my hair as my voice rises with each word. "You drive me fucking crazy!"

"Good. Someone has to."

Pressing my chest to hers, I continue to walk her backward. Eye to eye, nose to nose. "And you think it's your responsibility to do just that? You show up here unannounced and try to psychoanalyze me. And for what? Because we've both been through some shit?"

Her hand plants to my chest and she shoves me backward, drawing some space between us. "No. I showed up because you need someone and you have no one. Because when I needed someone, you were there. And I'm not talking about Josh's death. I'm talking about before he died. Come on, Zed. Don't act like you've forgotten."

Reclaiming the space I lost from her push, I look down at her. "Oh, I haven't forgotten. You crawled into my bed more times than I can count to get away from that psycho. I could never

RACHEL LEIGH

forget my first time, in the same way you can't forget yours. That's why you're here, isn't it? I thought I satisfied that need last night, but I take it you're hungry for more?" She pushes me again, but I eat the space right back up. Wrapping one arm around her waist, I pull her body flush with mine. "Is that it, Vienna?"

Her hand shoves my shoulder, but I don't budge. "Why do you keep calling me that? You know I hate it."

"Maybe that's why I do it."

"You would." She sneers. Her eyes peering up at me. I watch her lips as she talks. So soft and inviting. I can feel her heart beat against my chest as we stand molded together.

Unable to refrain any longer, my mouth crashes into hers. It's agonizingly satisfying. It's punishing and forceful, yet beautiful. My tongue sweeps around her mouth as if it's searching for something—clarity maybe. Her head angles to the side and I cup her cheeks in my hands. Just like our first kiss—just like our last.

Feeling her body shake in my grasp, I slide my hands down to cup her ass and scoop her up. Her legs wrap around me, her flip-flops falling off her feet, but neither of us pay them any attention as I carry her back to the house. Our mouths never parting, our hearts beating in sync while we share our breaths.

"Zed," she mutters into my mouth, "for my birthday..." She kisses me again.

"Your birthday has passed. But let's hear it," I grumble.

"I want you to fuck me again."

I pull back, looking her dead in the eye, wondering if I heard her correctly. Although, I'm not exactly sure what I was planning to do as I swept her up and carried her away, but I suppose that was a definite possibility.

She places her lips back on mine and I let her. I hate the hold she has on me. Most of all, I hate how much I love it.

I walk her up the steps and through the door. Carrying her into my room, I lay her on her back on the unmade bed. She kicks away the blankets as I collapse between her spread legs.

36

She's still wearing the same shorts she had on last night, but in a second flat, I rid her of them.

She should know I'm not gentle. I'm not sweet. If she wants this again, then she takes it the way I plan to give it to her, just like last night. I'm not the same guy I was our first time together years ago. I'll never be that guy again.

My lips glide down the nape of her neck until I reach her chest. Freeing her right breast, I suck her nipple between my teeth. Biting down with little pressure when all I want to do is devour every inch of her body like she's my last meal.

My cock hardens against the fabric of my joggers, and I'm, once again, pleased with myself.

Vi's hand snakes down between us and into the waistband of my pants, not stopping until she's squeezing my dick. She strokes up and down, with the little space she's given, while I dip two fingers inside of her.

I slide myself back up, taking her bottom lip in my mouth, and suck with tenacity. She cringes at the pain, but if I know Vi the way I think I do, she loves it. Pumping my fingers inside of her, I curl them and hit the spot that makes her hand tremble around me. She squeezes tighter, but stops stroking. Just holding my cock in her hand while her back arches into me. "You're soaking wet." I move down to her neck, sucking on the thin skin so hard that it's sure to leave a bruise.

She bucks up, and down, up and down, riding my hand as my fingers fuck her wet pussy. "Fuck me," she groans out of her dirty mouth.

Instead of giving her what she wants, I slide my body down until her hand breaks free, my cock missing her touch instantly. I tear my shirt off and toss it to the side. Her fingers slither up my ribs, leaving a trail of goosebumps in their wake. Once my face is level with her pussy, I dart my tongue out, sweeping up and down, tasting her sweet juices.

I stick one finger inside of her. Twisting and turning like a screw in a hole, and when I pull it out, I look up at her lust-filled eyes as she watches me. I pop my finger in my mouth and smirk. "Tastes like a legal pussy."

Her eyes roll, but I know my words turn her on even more. I stick my finger back in and this time, I'm not gentle. Another joins and I plunge them so far inside of her that my knuckles rim her entrance. Curling the tips, I pump continuously. Her legs fall completely to the sides and her mouth drops back open. Her eyes glossed over and wide as she pinches the bud of her nipple. "Uggh," she moans out. Throwing her head back while levitating her back off the bed. A second later, she spills around my fingers. Her arousal leaking out of her and onto the black sheet.

I pull my fingers out and begin rubbing vicious circles around her clit. Patting and vibrating them so fast that she screams out in pleasure. I don't stop. I move faster. Biting my lip in anticipation of her coming again.

When she does, her body jolts as if she's being zapped with a thousand watts of electricity. Her ass leaves the bed, and she slaps a hand over mine, stopping me. The heat suddenly more than she can handle.

Pushing myself up, I scan her expression for a reaction as I push down my joggers. Greedy eyes look back at me as I slide my body between her legs. Moving up, my dick goes right in. I give her a nanosecond to take a breath before my fingers wrap around the top of the headboard and I pound her pussy at lightning speed.

Her neck twists, resembling a pretzel as her head ricochets continuously off the upholstered frame while she keeps an eagle eye on me.

She brings both hands up and braces herself with her palms pressed to the frame to stop her neck from kinking further. I swoop an arm under her and slide her down, while still plunging my dick into her.

With my arm still sandwiched between her body and the bed,

I lift, bringing her chest closer to me. "Fuck," I wail. My head drops to her chest and I suck a nipple into my mouth. Not easing up, I graze my teeth on the thin skin. "You're gonna be the death of me, Vi." She's so tight and warm—dripping with arousal and the perfect fit for me.

I thrust once, twice, my body trembling and my heart hammering as my lungs attempt to inflate to no avail. My insides shudder before I fill up with an immense pressure. Grabbing my dick, I pull out as my chest rises and falls, pumping a couple times as my cum shoots all over her tits.

My hand drops and presses to the side of her rib cage. Lingering over her, reality slaps me in the face.

Twice in twelve hours. I did the one thing I swore I'd never do again. She's crawling back in like a spider, ready to make her web around me until she decides to leave for something better.

I push myself up without a word, feeling the dire need to get the hell out of here.

"Zed," she hollers as I give her my backside and walk out of the room completely naked. "What the hell?" she continues, her voice carrying down the hall as I enter the bathroom.

The door closes behind me and I head straight for the shower. Cranking it to freezing-ass cold, I climb in and let the water snap me out of my fucking stupidity. Last night was one thing. It was the heat of the moment. Maybe even for old times' sake. It meant nothing, absolutely nothing. Today was different.

This time, it was a big mistake.

CHAPTER SIX

There's no fighting the smile that creeps on my face. Granted, it doesn't mean anything at all, at least not to Zed, but it felt as amazing as last night.

It's been so long since he's touched me this way.

When I transitioned from a homeschooled student to a public school student, Zed and I became complete strangers. We'd pass in the hall like ships in the night. He still gave me butterflies and I often thought I did the same for him, but neither of us ever made it obvious—not the way we used to. Then he just...changed. His mom passed away and the Zed I knew was gone.

He wasn't exactly warm and fuzzy to begin with. Zed has always had a hard shell—traumatic experiences tend to raise walls—but he wasn't always so sad.

"So, who is it this time?" Zed asks as I stuff a handful of Cheetos in my mouth in the back of his pickup truck.

"Name's Luca," I say mid-chew with waggled brows. "He's got a killer tattoo of a tree with skulls that spreads the length of his arm. Apparently he was kicked out of three inner city schools before he thought the subs of Redwood were the right fit for him." I dig my hand into the bag and pull out another handful.

Zed lies back in the bed of the truck and gazes at the setting sun. "I'm sure he didn't make the choice himself."

"Probably not. He's pretty hot, though." My lips press together in a tight smile, knowing that my choice of words will warrant me a cynical outburst.

Zed springs back up, snatches the bag away from me and tosses it off the side of the truck. In two seconds flat, he's between my legs and my back is pressed to the rigid, tin bed. Grabbing my hand, he watches me intently as he hovers over my face. He pops my cheesy index finger in his mouth, sucking and feasting on my skin like it's an ice cream sundae. "He touches you, he dies."

"Like it matters. I'm nothing to you. Just a secret you like to keep."

His head drops down. His lips ghosting mine. Trailing over them in a tempting and seductive way that has my thighs clenching around his waist. "You're nothing to me, but everything at the same time."

"Yet, I made you my whole world."

"You're fifteen years old, you'll get over me. I promise. Besides, it has to be this way. Our paths were meant to cross, but we were never meant to stay on this road, Vi."

"Why?" I cry out. "Tell me why?"

"We've been over this. I'm too broken for you and you're too good for me."

"But, I'm broken, too. You make me feel whole, Zed, and I want you to be my first. My first everything and my only heartbreak. You're worth it to me."

"I'm nothing."

Tears prick the corners of my eyes when he talks that way. "You're so much more than you will ever believe."

His mouth falls on mine as though it's the first and last time, and I give him every ounce of me in hopes that it will make him feel whole—wanted, loved, and safe. I want him to break my heart so that it might mend his.

So I do. I give him my first time, and he gives me his.

Grabbing a pile of clean clothes from my bag, I make my way

to the bathroom. When I hear Zed huffing and puffing, I toss the clothes into the bathroom and keep walking to see what all the ruckus is about.

"Zed," I call out as I walk with hushed steps, my fingers trailing featherlike down the ivory-painted wall. My entire body tenses up, feet almost leaving the ground, when I hear the slamming of the front door.

He just needs a minute. I know he's feeling all the regret in the world right now. We were never supposed to connect in that way ever again. I really never thought we would.

There's some banging around outside that draws me over to the open window. *What the hell is he doing?* I stand there watching him, dumbfounded, as he kicks up dirt and throws his hands in the air. It's not until he spins around, his eyes landing on mine, that I realize he's on the phone.

Fast-tracked, I'm out the door with only a sheet wrapped around me. I hold tight to the corner of it, shielding my body as my bare feet pad against the wooden deck. I fly off the steps so fast that you'd think they were on fire. My hand descends toward him and I rip the phone away from his ear and out of his hand. Before he can say anything, I end the call without even checking who it was and then hold my finger down on the side button to power it off.

"What the fuck is the matter with you?" He reaches for the phone, but I hold it out until the screen goes black, then I let him take it.

"Who was that?"

His hand comes at me and I draw back, but he doesn't stop. His hand wraps around my neck, throwing me completely off guard. Cold fingertips press into my delicate skin as my pulse bobs against the palm of his hand. But that's not what startles me the most. It's the death glare laser-focused on me as his teeth bare down. "Mind your damn business, Vi. And don't ever pull that shit again." I grab his arm, but he doesn't budge until I squeeze his fingers and pry them off of me. He gives me a faint shove backward as his fingers untangle.

I heave, trying to catch my missed breaths. Grazing my fingers across the ghost of his grasp on my neck, I fume, "Fucking asshole." I punch his shoulder, but it doesn't faze him in the least. "Who was it? Was it one of them?"

Scowling, he walks past me, but I grab his arm. He shakes it off in a rapid motion, so I try again. "Did you tell them where you are? Are they coming here? Please, Zed. Tell me who it was." I can feel myself starting to panic. I should have known I'd be found eventually. I was just hoping I'd have a little more time to come up with a plan.

"It was Tommy. And no, he doesn't know where I am. But, get your ass dressed. We have to go back." He jogs up the stairs, leaving his words in the wind as if they have little to no effect on me.

"What?" I gasp, chasing after him. When he goes to close the door on my face, being the asshat that he is, I push it back open. "Are you crazy? We can't go back."

He scoops his keys off the counter and flashes me a look of superiority. "We can, and we will."

"Just take me to my car then. I'll leave and go somewhere else. I'm not going back to Redwood. Not now, not ever."

Orbiting around, his eyes fix on mine. "Where will you go?"

"Does it matter? An hour ago you didn't want me here."

"Fine," he deadpans.

"Fine?"

"Stay here. I'll only be gone for the day."

I wanna smile at his offer because it's a grand gesture coming from him, but the idea of staying here alone is terrifying. There isn't another house for at least three miles. It's secluded and kind of eerie, given everything that's going on. Zed said he was never going back either, but one call and he's ready to drive straight there.

"Why do you have to go back? What did he say?"

"Look, girl, I said you could stay, let that be enough. If it's not, then grab your overnight bag or whatever you came here with and see yourself out. Stay out of my business." He pushes the door open and doesn't give me a second look, or a chance to reply to his snide comment.

"What about my car?" I holler to him with no response back.

I'm not surprised because this is what Zed has always done. He spews off a bunch of words or threats and then walks away because he hates people and he hates talking. He's a private guy who prefers it when no one knows his business. A man of few words because too many might give the world insight into who he really is. One might say he's the devil, but I know better—I've seen his heart and heard it beat—he's just a lost boy.

I follow behind him, hugging the sheet tighter. "You'll be back, though, right?"

He pauses at his truck door, looking my body up and down before he speaks. "Yeah. I'll be back. Your car is fine. We'll get it tomorrow." Then he climbs in, brings the engine to life, and he's gone.

"Don't do anything stupid," I whisper into the exhaust he throws up behind him.

He says he's coming back, but can I trust him not to share my secrets before he does?

CHAPTER SEVEN

ZED

They can call me a snake, claim I'm cold and insensitive, but who's the first person to show up when they need something? Who is the one person who ignored all of his problems just to help them take care of theirs?

Me.

And the thing is, I don't even think they owe me for it because we're four friends who made a pact. I helped them, and in return, it's time for them to help me. They think I've settled my score because the satanic pastor is dead. What they don't know is that he wasn't my act. My target is still out there living his best life, when he's the sole reason mine fell apart.

I've known these guys since we were kids, but they don't know me at all.

"Waiting on a War" by Foo Fighters is interrupted when a call comes through. *Tommy* flashes on the screen and I tap *End*, returning to my music. I lean my head back on the headrest and immerse myself in the lyrics that are talking to me as an old friend.

"Why the hell do you even put up with the way he treats you?" I ask Mom as I hand her a glass of cold water. She pops a couple pills in her

mouth. Apparently her incision became infected and she's been put on a shitload of antibiotics.

"He only does it because he cares," she says, in reference to Dad. He's forced her to stay in this bed for months now, saying that she needs to rest to get well.

It's been two fucking months and it was a simple outpatient surgery. She was perfectly fine before she had her gallbladder taken out and now it looks as if she's disintegrating right in front of me.

"Yeah, well, I call bullshit."

"Zedulan Cane King, you watch that mouth of yours. You will not disrespect your father that way. He's a good man."

"Yeah, and he's got you fucking brainwashed," I mumble under my breath.

"I heard that, boy." She shifts on her side and turns to face me as I pace the length of her bedroom, gnawing on my thumbnail. "I know your dad can be a bit harsh—"

"A bit is an understatement."

"He works hard for this family and he's done a stellar job building his company from the ground up. Give him a break. Please. For me." She fakes a puppy dog frown, then smiles.

Mom is the only person in the world who gets me and loves me anyway. She knows how to calm me down, make me laugh, and she thaws out this ice-cold heart of mine. Sitting in front of me is the only person who will never give up on me. Without her, I'd have no one.

That woman had so much faith in me. Always saw the best in people, even the monster living inside her own house. He did this to her. He's the reason that she's gone.

Houses pass by all around me. Probably full of happy families with normal lives. Parents who love their children more than they love themselves.

Then there are the ones full of secrets and lies. Similar to mine. A mom who was sick and a father who kept her that way.

Not to mention, the abuse that happens outside of the homes that no one talks about because they fear they'll be ridiculed or shamed. A deep fear that the world will turn against them and look at them as if the acts were their own fault, just because they didn't fight back. Sometimes, we have to use all our strength on the inside, just to stay afloat, that we don't have any left to physically fight back.

I never told a soul about what that sick pastor did to me. I know I'm not alone. I know there were others, and I also know that they were all smiling on the day his rotting corpse was found. Just like I was. Just like *she* was.

My song is interrupted again. I end the call.

Just as the chorus begins, it cuts out...again.

My finger slams the touchscreen on the dash, accepting the call. "Damnit, Tommy. What the hell do you want now?"

"Just seeing if you're on your way."

"Really?" I huff. "You call three times just to see if I'm on my way when I told you ten fucking minutes ago that I was on my way."

"Alright, chill dude. See ya when you get here."

The call drops and my head shakes in complete and utter annoyance.

Just as it ends, another rings through. This is exactly why I've had my phone off for the majority of the last month.

This one, though, I take immediately.

"Hey," I say to the caller. An old man with a heart of stone and the voice of a robot.

"Look, kid. Your fun is over. Get your ass home and deal with your responsibilities or I'm canceling every card, phone, and insurance policy you have."

"You got it, Dad."

"Excuse me?" he says the words in a way that insinuates I insulted him by simply agreeing to his demands.

"I said you got it. I'm headed back to Redwood now."

His voice becomes tranquil. "Good. Come straight home. We have important matters to discuss."

And that call drops, too.

What's with people calling me and then being the ones to decide when the call is over?

More annoyance festers inside of me. I crank up the volume and let the music drown out the irrational thoughts seeping into my head. People fucking drive me crazy. Every single person in existence. Even Vi. Especially Vi.

There was a time when we were able to coexist. A time when nothing else mattered. We had a secret—I was hers and she was mine. But the thing with secrets is, they hurt you more than they protect you.

To this day, no one knows. But I do and I'll never forget.

"I thought I told you to stay away from her." I shove Luca in the chest. When he doesn't move, I shove him harder, over and over again, until his back hits the side of the house.

He laughs a mocking tone, then smirks, setting me off even more. I ball my fist, cock my arm and release. My knuckles penetrate the siding of the house, but I don't feel a thing.

"You're messing with the wrong guy, King. I could destroy you in two seconds flat."

"Oh yeah? Go ahead and fucking try."

"Go home, kid."

Nose to nose, I don't back down. "Maybe I am a kid, but so is she. Remember that next time you put your hands on her."

"It was a fucking hug. She was sad. Get over it."

"What's going on here?" Vi appears out of nowhere. She positions herself between the two of us, spreading her arms out to expand the distance as Luca and I stare each other down.

Luca points a finger at me, only provoking me further. "Your friend here was just coming to your rescue, thinking you need to be saved from me."

Vi turns to face me. Her cheeks tinged pink from the sun. "Go home, Zed."

I bring my hands to my chest. "Me? What the fuck did I do?"

*She grabs my arm and turns me around until I'm facing my house,
right next to hers. "You're looking for trouble where there is none. Now
go home."*

*My feet move as I glance at her over my shoulder. She's already
turned back to him. Laughing about something—probably me. Once I'm
at my house, I stop and look at them.*

*Luca throws an arm over her shoulder and leads her away while
they engage in a conversation that has her eyes lighting up. Vi stops. At
the same time my heart does. She grabs him by the arm and pulls his
face to hers.*

*Something unsettling swirls in my stomach. Is this what jealousy
feels like? My heart bends and snaps until it's completely broken in two.*

*This is the first time I've ever felt this way—and I can guarantee it
will be the last.*

That was the day she chose him. After everything we'd been
through. Countless nights of her sneaking in my room because
Josh was being a lunatic and breaking shit or threatening their
family. Her parents took his side just because they didn't want to
piss him off. Not to mention, the nightmares and lack of sleep on
both our parts because the horrors of our childhood still lived in
our heads. She got me, and I got her. She was ugly inside, just like
I was.

Vi can say that it was nothing personal. I was the one who
said we'd never be anything together. We were a dead-end road.
In exchange, she tossed me out and developed a new crush on
another guy who would also never be able to give her what she
wanted.

She chose him. A guy who was two years older than me. He
smoked cigarettes and drank from a flask. Was all set to start his
senior year at Redwood, but never did.

Because as fast as he came, he was gone.

∞

I PULL up to the four-thousand-square-foot box that I call home. Dad's slate gray nineteen-sixty-four Ferrari is parked out front and it immediately tells me he's in a good mood today. Funny how you can tell someone's mood just by the things they do that are out of the norm.

Dad only drives this prized possession for pleasure. Him seeking pleasure means he's not thinking business. Of course, that will all change when I walk through the door.

I hop out of my truck and close the door behind me. The smell of wet cement floods my senses and it isn't until I round the car that I see why. "Who the hell are you?" I snarl at a young blonde. She can't be a day over twenty-one. She's sporting a two-piece bikini, if that's what you'd call it. The bottom half is just a string of floss that her ass cheeks swallow up.

"Hey there. You must be Zed. I see good looks run in the family." She brings the hose up to her mouth and sticks out her tongue, licking the water like a thirsty dog.

My brows droop and if she thinks she looks sexy, she's dead wrong. "I asked who you were, not who I look like."

She pulls the hose away and lets the water flow down the dip between her breasts. "Sure is a hot day out here. Name's Dacey. I'm a friend of your dad's."

"Yeah, okay." I step past her and keep on my path to the front door.

Friend, my ass. She sure as hell ain't washing that car because she wants to earn a couple bucks. I go to open the door, but it opens for me. Dad steps out in a pair of Hawaiian print swim shorts and a tee shirt with a cigar tucked between his teeth. His salt and pepper hair is slicked back and the overpowering stench of his cologne is suffocating.

It's apparent the man is going through a midlife crisis.

"Son, you're home."

"Pretty sure I told you I was coming."

He steps out onto the large porch. "You did. I just wasn't

expecting you for a few hours. My last credit card statement showed you were somewhere called…Nanjunction."

"That's right. Small town outside of Brayburn. My own personal oasis. But, here I am, back in hell."

"Dacey," Dad calls over my shoulder. "Give me a few minutes, sweetheart. Water the lawn or something. I need to talk to my son." He grabs me by the shoulder and steers me inside.

Once we're in, he doesn't even close the door before he starts giving me shit. "I know you prefer to live like some punk-ass teenager, but that shit stops now. You already quit school and now you're running around the state pretending you own the goddamn place."

"Yes, sir." I nod in agreement.

He offers me an ear and bats his lashes. "Come again."

"I said, yes, sir. You're right. I've got something I need to finish up in Nanjunction and then I'll be back and ready to claim what's mine."

"What the hell are you talking about, boy?"

"My trust fund. I'm eighteen years old now. You might not know that because you missed my last four birthdays, but that was always the deal, was it not?"

"I know how fucking old you are. You quit school, Zed. You don't get a dime from me. And speaking of which, you are eighteen years old, about to turn nineteen, so you either finish and get your high school diploma or you hand over your cards and stop spending all my damn money."

"Is it, though? Is it really your money? Or was it Mom's?"

Dad's expression goes awry before he begins grinding his teeth and glaring at me. It seems I've hit a nerve with the puppeteer. The one who wants to control everything and everyone.

I step up to him with a locked jaw. My eyes zero in on his. "I'll be back, but I'm taking everything you fucking own, old man. Just like you took everything from us." My shoulder knocks his as

I walk past him to my room. I pull my phone out of my pocket and dial Tommy. When it goes straight to voicemail, I leave a message. "Be there in five. I'd prefer not to see Talon and Marni, so leave them out of this."

I push open the door to my room, which is just the way I left it, save the dirty laundry that was scattered all over the floor. It's now washed and sitting pretty on top of my dresser. Heading straight for my desk, I take out my keys and unlock my desk to retrieve the file of vile secrets. One I've held onto for over a year. I never planned to use it, but when Vi pulled me off that cliff, I knew I was kept alive for a reason.

All sinners have a past, but they don't all deserve a future.

Once I have the folder, I go out the same way I came in. Dad's perched in a chair puffing on his cigar while Dacey prances around his Ferrari with a soapy sponge. My eyes roll when I catch her looking at me while she squeezes the sponge over her tits.

I fucking hate people. Everyone is so eager to be seen and accepted. To look a certain way, to behave the way society wants them to—I refuse to do it. I am who I am and if they don't like it, then fuck them.

I've seen parents mold their children into who they want them to be from the minute they are born. They never get a chance to see the world through their own eyes because they're blinded by their parents' visions. We get money thrown at us for behaving as good little peasants. Graduate high school, go to college, take over the family business. Screw that. My dad didn't have to do all that. He just took it all from my mom and I'll be damned if he's gonna tell me how to live for a few million. I'd rather die poor before I did anything that bastard asked of me.

That won't happen, though. I have a plan and the guys and I have a deal. It's time they pay up, even if it costs them their souls.

"See ya around, *Dad*." I smirk devilishly, but he pays me no attention.

As soon as I'm in the truck, I toss the file in the passenger seat. The music blasting through the speakers continues and I drive away, for the first time in a while, feeling as if maybe there is light at the end of this tunnel. I've got a scheme in motion to take Dad out and a plan to end this madness with Josh.

I pull up to Lars' house where Tommy said they'd be. I sure as hell hope he got my message. The last people I wanna see are Talon and Marni. I'm still carrying a mountain of regret and a bad taste in my mouth after everything that happened. I tried for a while to forgive myself for what I did to her, but I just can't seem to get there, so expecting forgiveness from her is damn near impossible. As for Talon, I'm not sure that friendship can be repaired on either side. He hates me for what I did to Marni, and I hate that he let drugs control his life to the point that he was feeding them to others.

My feet hit the pavement with the file in hand and the front door of the house flies open. "Oh hey, Zed," Willa says as she wobbles in my direction.

My eyes pop wide open. "Wow. That thing ready to come out yet or what?"

"Believe it or not, I've still got three months," she shrieks. "I was just heading out to get some takeout from Scotty's. You want anything?"

"No, thanks. I don't plan on being here long."

"Alright. Guys are inside. It was good seeing you."

"Yeah, you, too." I force a smile on my face. Willa's a good girl. I have no problem with her. In a way, I sort of feel connected to her because she's seen the same darkness—even more so. Now, she's carrying proof of what that psycho pastor is capable of. But, I don't have ill feelings for the child. With Willa as her mom, the baby will be just fine. They don't know I know, but I do. The look on her face and lack of response when I asked a couple months ago told me all I needed to know.

I walk right into Lars' house and down to the family room in the basement. I'm not surprised one bit that the guys are engaged in an all-out war of COD. It's always been our thing, now it's just theirs.

"What's up, fuckers?" I throw my arms in the air. Not allowing them to see that I've been wallowing in self-pity while I've been away.

Lars throws his controller down and stands up. "Holy shit, he really is alive. Needs a trip to the dog groomer, but alive nonetheless."

"And you're about to have a baby and still living with your dad. Nice."

"Fuck you," he bellows. "I like the comfort of home."

"Annnnd, I see nothing's changed." Tommy walks over and slaps a hand in mine, then pulls me in for a hug. I give him an awkward clap to the shoulder, then step away.

"What the hell is he doing here?" I point at Wyatt McCoy sitting on the end of the couch. Last time I saw that guy, he was hysterical because he found Shane tied to a chair. It was an oddly satisfying moment.

"Oh, yeah. He's my boyfriend," Tommy spits out without taking a breath.

"Boyfriend, huh?" I nod. "Alright. I wondered when you were gonna step out of that closet."

Tommy raises a brow. "You knew?"

I look at Lars, then Wyatt, and back to Tommy. "Didn't everyone? You have a fucking Bruno Mars poster in your room and listen to Justin Bieber on replay. Not to mention, you were protective as shit over him."

Tommy chuckles. "Yeah, I guess I was." He looks over at Wyatt who smiles back at him. It's obvious they're happy and I wanna be happy for them. But for some reason, happy people remind me of how miserable my life is.

"Alright, now that that's out of the way, get rid of him. We need to talk." I drop down on the couch and kick my feet up on the coffee table in front of me.

"Sorry, Zed's sort of an asshole if you haven't noticed." Tommy gestures toward the stairs. "It'll only take a few minutes."

Wyatt rolls his eyes and gets off the couch. "Oh, I know exactly how Zed is. I think the entire town does."

I wait a second until the basement door closes, then shift upward and slam the file on the table. "Well, I'm glad everyone got their revenge and life is fan-fucking-tabulous, but guess what, boys? It's my turn."

"Wait a damn minute," someone behind me says. Not just someone—Talon. Where the hell did he come from?

My face drops in my hands. *Fucking great.* "Oh hey, good to see you, too." Sarcasm soaks my words.

"No, it's not. I don't wanna see you anymore than you wanna see me. Now what the hell are you talking about? The circle is closed. We finished the pact. We didn't call you here because we wanna do your dirty work. We called you here because the investigation is still open and we need to get ahead of things."

I jump to my feet and angle my head toward Talon. "What the hell do you mean, the investigation is still open? The pastor killed Josh, then he killed himself. The end. Case closed."

"It's not that easy. The autopsy report raised suspicion. The time of death and the drugs in his system. The case is still wide open and we need to get on top of it and talk to whoever did this before the cops find them first. We can't risk the truth coming out and then our part in everything being exposed."

"Okay. And what exactly do you suggest? We have no leads. We have nothing to go on." Vi said that the guys were after her. Could they really have reason to believe that Vi killed Josh?

"Vi Moran," Lars chimes in from behind me. I spin on my heels and question him with wide eyes. "We traced her on the app. She was using an anonymous name and after some digging, we found out that she was watching the dummy profile and Josh's."

I grimace. "Sounds like a coincidence to me. Why would Vi kill her own brother? It's stupid. Next suspect."

"Dude, it has to be her," Lars continues. "She went on the local news and tried to shift suspicion to Willa. Made it sound like Willa was having Josh's baby and that they ran off together. A guilty person tells lies."

I breathe out a hefty breath of air. "Yeah, you should know."

"What's that supposed to mean?"

I don't tell him that I know the baby isn't his. Wouldn't ever tell a soul, but everyone fucking lies. We're all lying to each other right now just to protect ourselves. That's what humans do to survive—they lie. "Nothing. But I think you're all wasting your time on Vi. Besides, is she even in Redwood anymore? Last I heard she took off."

Tommy steps forward with the remote in his hand. He mutes the TV, then drops the controller on the table. "Yeah, she took off because she's scared. If we can just find her and talk to her, we can get the truth and prepare for what comes next."

Anger boils inside of me. "You wanna fucking turn her in and throw her under the bus?"

"We wanna save our asses. But, no. We wouldn't turn on her unless she turned on us. If she goes to the cops and confesses that she did kill Josh, but has no idea how he got in the dead pastor's basement, then we have big problems."

Lars runs his fingers through his hair like he's getting stressed out already and I haven't even explained what I want yet. "Or she could know it was us all along and just spill it all."

Vi does know it was them. Vi and I both know the whole truth about what happened. These are my boys, but the backstabbing and the fighting have made me question where their loyalties lie. I've protected her this long; I'm not giving her up now. "Let it go, guys. You're driving yourselves fucking crazy. Creating scenarios in your heads and playing the 'what-if' game." I snatch the file off the table and open it up. A stack of papers stare back at me. Mom's hospital records, her death certificate, photos of Dad, photos of her, and even a photo of me.

Tommy lifts his chin. "What's that?"

"Everything we need for my act of revenge to play out. I don't need the 'no questions asked' rule because I'm gonna tell you everything you need to know."

"No," Talon shakes his head. "You got your fucking revenge. The pastor is dead."

My eyes lock on his, wide and ferocious, and laced with the full intention of doing whatever I have to do if he calls me out. "And what makes you think I killed that pastor? What gain would I have had?"

I know they all assume it was me, but none of them should know why it would be me. No one but Talon. Lars, maybe, because his girlfriend helped me retrieve the box. The same box that was lying next to his decomposing body. But what proof do they have?

Talon is at a loss for words as he looks around the room. "You...it had to be. Who else was it?"

My shoulders shrug. "Guess it was just our lucky day."

"So, you didn't do it?" Lars asks.

"Doesn't matter," I say matter-of-factly.

"And you're saying you have someone else that you want revenge on?" Tommy answers his own question before I can, "Of course you do. You have more enemies than Hitler."

"Yes. There is someone." I drop back down on the couch and shuffle through the papers while I speak. "You all know my mom died." I crane my neck to look at Talon behind me. "I'm not gonna rehash how she died, but I'm gonna tell you what happened before she died. Two years ago, she had a minor surgery. Gallbladder, I think it was. Got some pain meds, got better. You know how it goes. Only, she didn't stop taking the

57

pills." I hand Lars a picture of Dad dropping a pill in a glass of juice since he's the closest to me. "She didn't know it, but my dad was crushing them and putting them in her drinks. I think I counted three times a day to start. Then he started doing it more." I hand Tommy a picture next. "Once over-the-counter drugs weren't cutting it. My dad started getting the potent stuff. She still had no idea." Next, I hand Talon her medical records. "My mom was sick, but my dad was keeping her that way. One day, he stopped abruptly, and she damn near died. Dad gave her medicine and told her she'd be okay. And she was, but by then, she realized that she needed them all the time to feel good. He got her addicted and he is the one who paid the dealers. He made all the calls and set up all the deliveries. Except for one."

The room grows silent and Talon knows exactly which one I'm talking about. The final delivery. The final pills. The ones that she took to purposely end her life because she couldn't feed the addiction anymore. It was too much for her that no drug was enough.

"Everything my father owns is because of her. You all know who my grandfather was. He left everything to his only child— my mom. A fortune big enough to buy an entire continent. Dad was a measly stock broker when they got married. He did this for money. And now, I'm taking that money back." My grandfather was the president and CEO of one of the biggest oil companies in the world. He died before I was born, so I never knew him, but I know that he adored my mom.

"Shit, man, I had no idea." Lars hands me back the picture. Followed by the others. I stuff them back in the file and set it on the table.

"I didn't either until I spent the first six months after her death reviewing every second of camera footage in the house. Once I saw that first pill dropped in her drink, I searched harder. I got footage from the pharmacy. I contacted dozens of dealers within a ninety-mile radius. And in the end, I got the truth."

"Why didn't you ever tell us?" Tommy asks with sincerity in his tone.

"Why doesn't matter. But I'm ready to come back to it, and you guys are gonna help me." The truth is, so much shit started happening after my mom died that I figured it was pointless to even try and take my dad down.

"And what if we say no?" Talon barks from behind me, sending me to my feet in one second flat.

His words set me off. That fire inside me burning hot as my back steels and my chest bumps his. "Then I'd have to call you a little bitch for backing out of a pact that we made in blood. I helped you, now it's your turn to return the favor."

Bumping me back, trying to act all tough, Talon tips his chin and looks down on the extra inch of height he has on me. "I think the favor was returned to you when you helped yourself to my girlfriend."

"You're still crying about that shit?" Bad choice of words on my part.

I'm mid-blink when Talon shoves me back so hard that I flip over the couch. I get right to my feet as he hustles around the couch with balled fists and a look of pure insanity on his face. "You're fucking dead." He charges at me, but this time, I'm prepared.

I crouch down and tackle him at the waist. Lifting up, and slamming his body into the cushions. "You're right. I am fucking dead. So nothing you do can hurt me. Give it your best shot." I slap a hand to my cheek. My jaw clenched as heavy breaths fume from my nostrils.

I just stand there like a stone statue as Talon lands his fist on my cheek. My head snaps to the side, but I bring it right back, front and center. Then he smacks my other cheek. "That all you got?" I breathe heavier, relishing in the pain.

Another blow to the other cheek. I don't falter. I stand there, taking what's being given, because I deserve it.

"Fucking stop it!" Lars bellows, grabbing Talon from behind.

Tommy comes to my side. "You okay, man?"

I mean, it's not really a normal gathering among me and the guys if one of them doesn't come at me.

I spit out some blood directly on the coffee table. "Fucking great." Bending down, I snatch up the folder and leave the basement without another word.

Truth is, I have a mountain of regret over what I did. Marni might not have stopped me, but I didn't seek her approval either. I was in a bad place and I was fucked-up that night. Could barely even think straight. I remember looking at her and being so drawn to her because she reminded me of Vi. Her hair, her eyes, her frame, and the way she carried herself. She exuded confidence and had a 'take no shit' attitude. I knew she was into Talon, but I thought that maybe if she were into me, I could like her back. Maybe then I could erase the memories of the one I really wanted.

With a bobbing head and legs that can barely hold my weight, I push open the door. There she is. Beautiful and innocent. Like she laid in that bed just so I could come in and cloak her body with mine.

She's still. Not even a breath can be heard. Slow steps lead me to her side and my ass sinks into the plushness of the mattress. Her body tenses up and when she goes to speak, I put a hand over her mouth. Her warm breath coats my palm with dampness.

She puts up a fight and tries to free herself from my touch. Like I'm the monster of the night who came to take her soul.

"Surprise, Little Thorn," I whisper the words in her ear, but I cannot fully comprehend what I'm even saying, let alone what I'm doing.

I lean close, my face level with hers as my cheek brushes the nape of her neck. Her breath hitches and I can almost hear the thudding of her heart when my fingers snake up to her mouth and I trace the outline of her perfect lips. With a sweep of her hair, I push it to the side and rest my chin on her shoulder and droop down until I'm lying on top of her.

"Talon's in here. He'll wake up, and he'll be pissed," she says with no attempt to quiet her voice.

"Talon. Talon. Talon. It's always fucking Talon. He's asleep, which you already know. Don't you know that you should never drug a druggie?" She thinks I didn't see, but I see everything. I'm not sure how many pills she gave him, but it was apparently enough to knock his ass into a comatose sleep.

I don't know why she even wants this guy. He is, in fact, a druggie. One that fed his own addiction while keeping my mom content in hers.

Marni can do so much better, just like Vi could have done so much better. But they both chose the wrong men, neither chose me.

Vi.

My Vienna.

Why is she still so heavy on my mind after two fucking years? I can still smell the sweet vanilla scent of the body spray she'd put on every morning.

No matter how hard I try to rid my mind of that girl, I can't. She walks the halls of Redwood as a stranger obeying my demands. She doesn't even look at me, because I told her not to. Was I foolish to make such a lifelong demand because of my temporary pain? Now, I'm too stubborn to recant what I said, all because my pride is as big as my ego.

Marni can make me forget.

"No one was supposed to touch you outside of that one video. But Talon did, didn't he?" We made a deal—one he broke. It's just like Talon to go back on his word, time and time again. Yet, they make me out to be the bad guy all because I call them out on their shit.

She gasps when my fingers slide inside of her. Twisting and turning, poking and prodding.

Her body slides up, but my fingers remain packed tightly in her pussy. "How do you know all of this stuff about me?" She whimpers.

"I'll tell you," my teeth graze her cartilage, "but not until I finish you off. I want you to come so fucking hard that it gushes."

She doesn't stop me. She wants this just as much as I do. She's going to love me one day. Then, and only then, can I unlove Vi.

"Come for me, Marni. I know you want it."

I sit up, straddling her legs, and decreasing the intensity. Two fingers slide in and out while I use my other hand to rub against her clit. She moans and arches her back in unison.

She fucking loves it.

"You like that, don't you?" I say in a throaty roar.

"Don't fucking talk." Her hips buck up, wanting more.

"Oh yeah," I moan, *"you're soaking wet for me. Just for me."*

"You're fucking sick." She cries out as she begins to clench around my fingers. Riding them out until I make her come. Her arousal surges down the joints of my knuckles and I pull my fingers out.

I press a chaste kiss to her cheek and whisper, *"I am sick, but you drugged the guy you care about and let me shove my fingers in your pussy while he slept on the floor."*

As I'm walking out to my truck, my phone buzzes.

Talon: Help us, and we'll help you. Find Vi.

CHAPTER EIGHT

I've paced the length of the house for the past two hours, trying to decide if I should go get my car and leave before they come for me. I can't pretend that I can trust Zed. Everyone that knows him is well aware that he can be pretty selfish when it comes to getting what he wants—scratch that, not pretty selfish, very selfish.

I hold my finger down on the power button on the side of my phone, bringing it to life. I don't hesitate before pulling up the Uber app. If I'm going to do this, I have to do it quickly before my phone can be traced. I search for drivers in the area and when the loading button circles around continuously, my nerves begin to get the best of me.

"Come on," I mumble as I tap the ball of my foot repeatedly to the floor.

One minute later, 'no results' shows on the screen. I should have known that there wouldn't be any drivers in the area. We're practically in the middle of nowhere. I'm not even sure what the name of this town is. I only have one option left—get a taxi from the city.

I pull up Google and do a search for a company within a thirty-mile radius. *Nothing.*

My car is literally three miles away, and by the time a taxi gets here from Brayburn, Zed could be back, and he could have company with him.

Walking is pretty much my only option at this point. It would take me forty minutes tops.

Before I can turn my phone off, a call comes through. *Mom* flashes on the screen, and I cringe at the sight of her name. *What the hell does she want?*

Against my better judgment, I take the call. "Yeah, Mom. I'm fine," I say, before even letting out a breath and allowing her to greet me with a hello.

"Vienna Moran, don't you get snippy with me."

I didn't. Nor did I plan to, but Mom takes any preconceived notions as an insult.

"Sorry, Mom. How are you?" My eyes roll as the words leave my mouth.

"Have you talked to Principal Burton? You said you handled this and you were all set to switch to virtual enrollment." She cuts right down to business. No 'how are you?' or 'are you safe?'

"Yes," I lie.

Mom huffs, like I'm wasting her precious time. "Then why did I get another call today?"

"I dunno, Mom. Maybe she forgot."

"Call her today. If I hear from her again, you will be coming home and going back to in-person schooling. No child of mine will be a high school dropout."

Unlucky for her, I'm the only child left.

"Okay, I'll call her now," I say, getting bored with this conversation.

"I mean it, Vienna." Her tone is stern. "There are only three months left of the year. Finish them out."

"Okay, Mom!" I spit out harshly. "I have to go." The more time

I'm on this phone, the more time they have to track me down. I know that Wyatt is fully capable of finding out where I am.

"Do what I said. Goodbye," she says before the call drops.

She'll forget all about this until the next call from Principal Burton.

Her call to me is a reminder that I'm alone in this world. When it all comes down to it, I only have myself. I'm an inconvenience to my parents, I was always an embarrassment to Zed, and no matter how hard I tried to make friends, it never stuck.

Zed might think he's alone, but deep down, he has to know that Tommy, Lars, and Talon would do just about anything for him. He might be the outcast of the group, but there is no doubt in my mind that they have each other's backs. Friendships get shaky, relationships turn sour, but everyone with a shared past is bonded in one way or another. Just like me and Zed. No matter how much he tries to deny the fact, we are connected forever.

I go into the room I claimed as my own for my short stay and dig in my black overnight bag for a pair of jean shorts and a black crop top. I change quickly, then grab my Air Force One sneakers. They're all white and sure to be trashed by the time I finish my walk, but it's better than the alternative of open-toed flip-flops. I shuffle through my bag, then remember I left my flip-flops outside when they fell off my feet.

Once I'm dressed, I stuff my dirty clothes into my bag and zip it up. There's no way in hell I'm carrying this thing, so I'll have to come back for it once I get my car. I pick it up and carry it outside, then drop it on the porch, so I can just grab it and go once I have my car.

Then, I have no choice but to leave. Probably stay at the hotel in the city I was in for the last week while I waited and watched for the most opportune time to make my presence in the area known to Zed.

It all started as me hiding out. But once I saw the state of mind Zed was in, everything changed. As much as I hate the way things fell apart, I don't like seeing *him* fall apart. He's too strong for that. He's been through too much to give up now.

We both have. Which is exactly why I have to leave. I can't stay here and try to save him at the risk of sinking myself.

Fortunately, he seems to have snapped out of whatever misery he was in because the way he rushed out gave me the inclination that he's up to something. He has unfinished business of his own.

∞

IF I WOULD HAVE TAKEN another minute to think about things before rushing out, I would have realized that bringing something to drink would have been a fabulous fucking idea. I'm only about a mile in and I'm already parched. We're in the midst of a dry spell and fires in the area have been at an all-time high. There's a smog that lingers over everything like a blanket beneath the clouds. My nostrils feel dried out, my throat feels coarse, and even my lungs feel heavy.

The only good thing about this walk is the fact that I have yet to see a car. It's like a ghost town with no town. Just dirt roads and houses that are miles apart.

Stopping for a minute, I turn my phone on just to check my location. I'm pretty sure it was a straight shot, if I remember right. I tap my map app and look at the geographical icon for Rubble Edge. It looks so close on the map, but I'm still over two miles away. Sighing heavily, I turn my phone back off.

Kicking up gravel and dirt beneath me, I try to just take in my surroundings. I've always loved the quiet. In such a noisy world, it's hard to find peace and solitude. The only downfall—you're then left with only your thoughts.

My eyes are still closed and my lips are still puckered when Luca places his hands on either side of my shoulders. "No, Vi." He pushes me away. Not in a rude way, but in an 'I'm too old for you' way.

My eyes open and I wear my humiliation in my expression. "But I thought you liked me."

Luca chuckles dryly, making me blush even more. "You're only fifteen years old. I'm a senior in high school. Besides, I'm not good for you, baby girl. I'm just here for a short while."

I take a step back, observing the gorgeous, ruffled guy in front of me. "Oh yeah? How long of a while?"

His shoulders shrug. "Till I do what I came to do." He slides his cheap black shades down. His beautiful blue eyes are now covered by the lenses. His lip tugs up in a sly smirk that sends a new wave of emotions running through me. I'm not sure if it's excitement at the challenge, or sadness that I'll never win.

It's fractions compared to the way I felt about Zed, and again, I lost. Zed has made it clear that I'll never have a place in his heart. To him, I'm just the girl next door who knows too much. He's probably just nice to me because of that fact.

Just as I go to speak—wanting to tell Luca I'm sorry for throwing myself at him like a little floozy—Josh comes around the corner. His heavy brows dipped into an angry v and his shoulders drawn back. "What the fuck is going on over here?"

Luca doesn't drop his smug look and I can't help but get the feeling these two have already had their first encounter since Luca arrived yesterday. "Just getting to know my new sis." He throws an arm over my shoulder and pulls me close until the side of me is snugly beside him.

"Eighteen years old and kissing a fifteen-year-old girl. What kind of sicko are you?" Josh snarls with a curled lip.

"He didn't kiss me," I chime in. "I kissed him and he pushed me away." I shouldn't have said anything. I'm sure I'll pay for it later with broken objects in my room, holes in the wall. That's Josh's MO. He doesn't hurt me physically; he tries to break me down emotionally. Not just me, my parents, too.

"Not what I heard." He points up toward Zed's house.

My heart sinks into my stomach. Like an anchor getting dropped from a boat. Zed stands at the window shirtless. His prominent abs on full display. But that's not what catches my eye. It's the middle finger he's holding up while looking me dead in the eye.

He saw me kiss Luca.

"In the house. Now," Josh says, before walking away and leaving me and Luca alone—aside from Zed still staring at us.

Luca goes to walk away, but I step in front of him. "What is it that you came here to do?"

He doesn't even hesitate before speaking. "I came here for Josh."

I'm lost in my thoughts and don't even realize it when I come to the two-track drive of Rubble Edge. Taking a left, I keep walking. I parked off to the side when I came here yesterday, because I suspected Zed was here for a reason. He's not one to just go somewhere and collect his thoughts. He's either hiding out or he's plotting. In this case, he was plotting, but it wasn't the demise of another; it was his own death.

The closer I get to my car, the more anxious I feel myself getting. I catch sight of the glimmering black bumper. Something strange washes over me. The feeling that I'm being watched. I spin around quickly, my eyes darting around the weathered landscape. I didn't even realize I was holding my breath until I released pent-up air. I take a few more steps, the unease growing greater.

With my last step, my stomach twists in knots when I see him leaning on the trunk—arms crossed over his chest and the scowl he wears so well hanging tightly to his face. "What are you doing here?" I ask, playing it off like I'm not completely shocked to see him. Like I wasn't planning to get my car to run away because I fear that he's given me up to his friends.

"I could ask you the same thing. Thought you were staying. It's what you wanted, isn't it?"

"I umm...I was worried someone would find my car. Trace the plates and contact my parents." I walk casually over to the driver's side door. I go to open it, but it's locked. I pat my shorts and fuck if I didn't leave my keys on the dresser in that room. "Damnit," I spit out.

I look over at Zed when I hear the clanking of keys. He's holding them up, dangling them in the air. "Looking for these?"

Taking a step toward him, I go to snatch them out of his hands, but he retreats. His hands drop and he takes a step back. "Where ya going, Little Lamb?"

"How'd you get those?"

A menacing laugh climbs up his throat. "You walked all this way with no fucking keys?" It's apparent he finds my lack of preparedness funny.

"I was in a hurry." I try to snatch them away again.

His tone shifts to a serious note when his humored expression drops instantly. "Get in the truck, Vi."

"What? No!" I spit out. "I came for my car and I'm leaving with my car." Is he serious right now?

He takes a step toward me, his hand rises to my face, and the back of his fingers brush my cheek. "Were you planning on leaving?"

Chills shimmy downward from his touch. "I told you, I just wanted my car." I chuckle nervously. "I can't just leave it here."

"Sure ya can. No one knows it's here. No one will find you. Don't you trust me?"

I raise a brow, peering up at him. "Should I?"

There's a beat of silence as tension coils between us and the only sound is the thudding of my heart in my chest.

"You're the one who tells all the lies. Maybe it's time I play a little game of my own."

He doesn't have to go into detail. I know exactly what he's talking about. It's been three years and even though I've been stuck in that day, I thought he moved on from it. He dropped me like a sack of potatoes, and while I was sure neither of us had any anger toward the other, I'm starting to second-guess that assumption.

"I was fifteen years old, Zed. You were only sixteen."

"Did I not have feelings then, Vi? Did I not have a heart?" His nostrils flare as he grows angrier. I need to defuse this bomb before it goes off. Zed can go from chill to explosive in a matter of seconds. I know he'd never hurt me physically, but his words can be harsh—his demands insensitive.

"I don't know how many times I have to tell you that Luca meant nothing to me. Besides, he's dead. Remember?"

His cold fingers hit my cheek again as he tucks my hair behind my ears. "New tattoo?" he asks, changing the subject completely. I know he remembers, but no one has even mentioned Luca's name since the day he died. It's like he never even existed aside from that brief moment when Zed thought I was choosing Luca over him. The days that followed were painful and real.

"I got it a couple months ago," I tell him, in reference to the black butterfly with a broken wing behind my ear. My eyes shift downward to his hand that's clenching my keys. "Are you planning on giving those to me?"

Still looking at my tattoo, he completely ignores my question. "Why did you get it?"

I scoff. "I don't know. I liked it, I guess." I lay my open palm out to the side of us. "Would ya give me my damn keys?"

"What broke your wing, Vi?"

I give him my truth. "Everyone."

"Me included?"

"Especially you. Didn't you ever notice the way I looked at you? Like you hung the fucking moon. But you wanted to hide me away, just like my mom did."

He comes up behind me. His body flush with mine as he sweeps my hair over my shoulder to one side. "I never wanted to hide you. I wanted to protect you."

"Right," I nod with sarcastic flare, "because it was safer for me to be stuck at home with my deranged brother and pretend like I didn't have the same fucked-up childhood you did."

"We couldn't coexist, Vi. Not in front of the world. Not with everything we'd been through." In the same breath, his tone shifts. "But, none of that matters. The monsters aren't hiding under our beds anymore."

"Maybe not under yours, but your friends are after me."

"Don't fret, I'm the only one who knows all your secrets." He comes forward, his cheek brushing mine as his lips trail feather-like against the lobe of my ear. "Now I need to know why I should keep them to myself."

"What do you want from me, Zed?"

"Not a damn thing. You came to me. So the question is, what do you want from me, Vi?"

What do I want? His silence. The comfort of knowing that nothing I did will ever see the light of day. I want his protection because he's the only one in the world who has ever made me feel safe. Most importantly, I want him to be okay. As strange as things have been between us, I can't live in this world without him.

But I don't tell him any of that because Zed gets uncomfortable when it comes to emotions. "I need you to promise me that you'll never tell a soul what happened."

"Beg for it."

"What?"

"Get on your knees and beg for the promise."

I chuckle nervously. "I'm not getting on my knees and begging."

"Then I guess you don't want it bad enough."

I stand there for a minute, watching him and waiting to see if he's serious, but, of course, he is. Zed is a grade-A asshole.

My arms fly up. "Fine. You want me to beg? Fine." I drop to my knees, knowing I have nothing to lose except my pride.

"Would you please promise me that you will not tell the guys what I did?"

Bending down, he grabs my hand, he peels my fingers back one at a time while his eyes are level with mine. When my keys drop into my hand, I look down and he closes my fingers around them. "Go back to the house. Bring your bag back inside, and don't leave. If you do, I will find you."

He turns around to go to his truck without even giving me a second look.

"You didn't promise," I holler over my shoulder. He keeps walking, leaving me on my knees in the sand, looking like a damn fool.

Glancing down at my hand, I can feel his touch lingering but slowly fading, leaving behind an emptiness. It's the same feeling I got a couple years ago. Every time I'd sneak in his house and lay in his bed with him, he'd wrap his arms around me to make me feel safe. When Josh would have crazy mood swings and start breaking shit or threatening us, Zed was my safe place.

He never told anyone about the dysfunction of my family. He was just...always there. Until the sun came up and he'd sneak me back out before anyone could see. He didn't want the world to associate us because of our past. Zed thought that if I came out about what happened with the pastor, he'd be found out, too. His faith in me has always been miniscule, but I don't take it personally. Zed doesn't trust anyone, not even himself. I've always wanted to love him enough for the both of us, but he'd never let me. He's a broken boy with a past that haunts him. He's my broken wing.

CHAPTER NINE

ZED

The first time I saw Vi, she was this ten-year-old firecracker, with jet-black hair that reached the middle of her back. She stood in front of a U-Haul truck at the house next door to mine, refusing to let the movers get her stuff out. She didn't want to move to this town and she made it known. I watched her from my window expecting her to cry, but she never did. She didn't throw a fit, never raised her voice. She just spread her arms and told them her belongings were going back to her old house.

She's always been so good at holding in her emotions while making her demands obvious. Those big burly men were scared of that little shit. It wasn't until her dad scooped up her stiff body and carried her away that they were able to do their job.

Vi has taught me so much over the years, just by observing her from afar. I knew what was going on in that house long before she told me. Josh was a menace. He was dangerous and unpredictable behind closed doors. He was abusive to his parents and he'd beat Vi down emotionally. I wanted to protect her, but it wasn't long before I realized that Vi didn't need protection. She knew how to take care of herself all along.

I pull up to the rental house, shift into park, and wait. I could have followed her to make sure she'd come back, but I knew she would. For the first time ever, Vi is scared. For good reason, too.

Now I have a decision to make. Keep protecting her, or let the guys do what they want with the information I can give them. Until I decide, I need to keep her at arm's reach.

My life has always been like an open circle and until it closes, I'll never feel free to be happy. Bad shit just keeps coming through the cracks. I thought the pastor's death would close it, but it didn't, which sent me into a dark place; a place I feared I'd never crawl out of alive.

It wasn't until Vi showed up and pulled me away from that ledge that I realized I stayed alive for a reason. Dad is the missing link. The one who started this ripple in my life. He's the one who needs to pay for his sins. Maybe then, I can forgive myself for mine.

As I'm waiting for Vi, a call comes through from Tommy. I should have known once I turned my phone on that I'd have to deal with constant calls from him. Tommy and I have become the closest out of the guys and he's the only one I really care to talk to anymore.

I tap the answer button on the screen. "Yeah," I deadpan.

"Hey, man. That was some craziness I didn't expect today."

"Really?" I raise my voice. "I made it perfectly fucking clear that I didn't want him there. You didn't for once think that I said it for a reason?"

"We didn't know he was coming. He just sort of showed up."

I sigh heavily. "What's done is done. What do you need, Tommy?"

"I wanna help you," he tells me point-blankly.

My neck draws back in surprise. "You do?" Since when does anyone *want* to help me?

"Yeah. You helped all of us in your own crazy way and I owe it to you. You dropped everything to come help me with Shane. You were there for all of us when we needed help."

He's right, I was. Because above all, I keep my word. "I'm coming back into town this weekend. We can go over the plan then."

"Lars and Talon are in, too. They just wanna find Vi first."

Running my fingers through my hair, I sigh heavily. "They're not giving this up, are they?"

"It makes sense, though. She was on the app and everything points to her. They're hellbent that she has all the answers we need to end this shit."

"Doesn't make any sense. None of us have ever even talked to Vi Moran."

"Well, they've pulled Wyatt into this and he was able to ping a location on her phone from earlier today. They're actually following a lead right now, so we—"

"Hold up. What?" My head shoots up as I look down the driveway to see if she's coming. When I don't see her, I start my truck back up and slam into drive and whip out of the driveway. I keep Tommy on the call to try and find out where they might think she is.

"Couple hours away. Wyatt's here with me, but Talon and Lars are following up on it. They might not even need you."

"I gotta go." I end the call abruptly.

Fuck!

Completely ignoring the speed limit, I haul ass down the road, kicking up gravel behind me. Calling her is pointless because she knows better than to have her phone on. At least, I thought she did.

Damn that girl! She must have turned it on at some point. Doesn't she know by now that they have a tech geek on their side tracking and tracing everyone's moves?

Good thing is, they don't give a shit enough about me to even try and find out where I am. Not sure if I should be glad or severely disappointed in the fact that my childhood friends can barely stand to be around me.

My foot slams the brake to the floorboard when I see Vi's car coming down the road toward me. She stops parallel to me and rolls her window down. "What now?" She pushes her shades on her head.

"Go into the city and take the first exit. There's a hotel that sits back off the freeway—The Hilton, I believe. Check in under my name and I'll be there later."

"What the hell are you talking about?"

"Just do what I said. And do not," I emphasize, "do not turn your phone on. If you get lost, stop and ask for directions." I can feel panic ensuing and, once again, I fucking hate the hold this girl has on me. Why do I have to be her savior when she's done nothing for me? Sure, she thinks she saved my life, but did she really? Or was she just saving her own ass once again?

Her brows shoot to her forehead. "Why? What have you done, Zed?"

"Just go." I push on the gas and whip a U-turn in the middle of the road, then follow behind her while she creeps at the speed limit. My open palm smacks the steering wheel and I hang my head out the window and shout, "Would you fucking speed up?"

I know she didn't hear me, but she can see the displeasure in my expression from her rearview mirror and responds with her middle finger out the window.

She's beyond infuriating and every snide remark or turbulent gesture brings out the worst in me—but the best at the same time, if that's even possible.

I pull up to the house, and there they are. Talon and Lars stand with their asses resting on the bumper of Lars' car. My entire body itches at the unwanted stares they're offering me.

I immediately notice Vi's bag flung over Talon's shoulder.

Eight years of secrets with this girl. A girl no one knew existed until her brother died. A girl that no one knows I even know. And this is how it all comes out. Not only do I know Vi Moran. She knows me—the only person in the entire world who does. She knows every scar, every loss; she saw the only tears that fell from my eyes.

Alright. This is fine. They have nothing.

I draw in a deep breath, ready to take what's bound to be thrown at me. "Hey, guys," I say casually. As if their presence at my secret hideout has no effect on me.

"What are you doing here?" Lars asks.

My hands go up. "Surprise."

"You're telling me you're staying here, too?" He digs deeper, unsatisfied with my response. "With Vi?"

"What makes you think Vi is here?" I play dumb.

Talon swings the bag around and drops it on the ground in front of him. He quirks a brow. "How about this?"

My shoulders waggle as I make my way over to them. I'm sure they've riffled through the bag and are well aware that it doesn't belong to me. "What can I say, the ladies love me. Even in the middle of buttfuck Egypt, they come to see me."

"Cut the bullshit. What are you doing here and where is Vi?"

"To the left of U and next to W." When they don't catch on to my terrible joke, Talon stalks toward me with a puffed-out chest. I give him a shove before he even has a chance to do whatever the hell he planned to do.

"This isn't a fucking joke. Have you been helping this girl?"

Lars just lingers behind him, unsure what to make of all this. Something catches his eye and he wanders away, but I regain my focus on Talon. "Why is everyone so damn concerned with what I do all the time? You all really need to get a hobby."

Talon scoffs. "You do realize all you're doing is making her look guilty as hell?"

More likely than not, he's probably right. Doesn't matter, though. Personally, I don't give a fuck what anyone thinks. The fact of the matter is, even if they did find out what really happened that night, they can't do shit. We're all guilty. We would all face serious charges. This isn't about them wanting to find the killer; this is about them wanting to protect themselves.

"You really need to let this shit go. I've told you all, time and time again, that it's over. Just enjoy life." I go to slap a hand to his back, but he swats it away. "You've fucking changed, man," I spit out before actually spitting on the ground near his feet.

"And you haven't. But maybe it's time you do. We're all growing tired of your games, Zed."

Reality should slap me in the face right about now—because he's right—but it doesn't. It's true that I'm my own worst enemy. "If I remember right, you started these games. All because you wanted to coerce Marni into loving you." I start clapping with a shit-eating grin. "Bravo. You got the girl."

His lips twitch with humor. "That's right, I did. And you didn't."

My shoulders rise with a scathing frown. "Didn't want her anyway. She reminded me of someone I once knew. She had the same tight pussy—wet and willing. Just the way I like 'em."

Talon's palms shove against my shoulders before he tries to swing me around and wrap his arm around my neck. I'm a little too quick for him, and slither right out of his reach. An airy laugh leaves my vocal cords as I slap my hands to my chest. "We can go all night. Show me what else you got."

He shakes his head with a tsk to his tongue. "I can't believe I ever called you a friend. You're fucked in the head."

"Ditto, dickhead. In fact, I wish we never were friends." My voice rises to a high-pitched shout. "Maybe then I wouldn't care so much that you killed my fucking mom."

"For the last time, I didn't know. How many times do we have to go over this?"

"And how many times do I have to tell you that I was fucked-up and thought Marni wanted it?"

"Never," he says matter-of-factly.

I tip my head. Unsure what he means. "Never?"

"You never told me that. Never even tried to explain what happened. You just used your humorous asshole tendencies to make yourself feel better. Never once tried to help anyone understand."

I sweep the air with my hand and turn around. "What's the point? No one fucking cares what I have to say." Lars starts coming back toward us with something in his hands.

"As deranged as you are, you've helped us all a hell of a lot. I would have listened. Probably wouldn't have mattered much, but I'd at least hear you out."

What the fuck is Lars holding?

Talon keeps talking, but I'm more focused on what Lars has in his hand. "Are you even listening to me?"

As Lars comes closer, I start to make out that he's holding a pair of flip-flops. He holds them up in the air. "Does anyone know who wears black flip-flops with white skulls on the straps?" When we don't answer, he answers his own question. "Vi. That's who."

"Pretty sure we already established that she was here." I look around the property, playing dumb. "We must have just missed her. Damn girl probably broke into my house and slept in my bed. Ate my porridge, too."

Lars slams the flip-flops to my chest and I let out a muffled groan. I snatch them up before they fall. "Not really my size, but thanks."

"Where is she?"

I hold up the shoes with a smirk. "Wherever she is, she's barefoot."

Lars huffs and looks from me to Talon. "This is a waste of time. He's not on our side. Never was."

I should say something. Anything to assure them that some-where inside of me is the friend they once knew, but the words are so far out of my reach that I can't even begin to throw together a sentence. *I am on their side.* These are my boys, my friends, the only family I have—aside from Grandma; they're the only ones who have cared. They get cut, I bleed. I'd do fucking anything for them. But why can't I say it to their faces?

"Yeah, let's go," Talon says. They give me one last look as I stand there with a blank expression and nothing left to say.

As they walk away, I internally scream at myself to stop them. Say something. Do something.

Fuck. What is the matter with me?

"Wait," I spit out. They both turn to face me and I give the shoes in my hand a toss to the side. "If you help me take down my dad, I'll help you get the answers you need. All of them. We can end this all. For good this time."

They share a look as if they're speaking to each other without words. Talon looks back at me. "What do you need us to do? Bury a body? Or something simpler like throwing a party?"

My head shakes no. "There will be no bodies. My act is short and sweet. I don't want the old man dead. I prefer that he lives a miserable life of regret and shame. I wave my hand over my shoulder, gesturing for them to follow. When they don't, I glance over my shoulder. "What the fuck are you waiting for? Come on."

There's some huffing and puffing and probably some silent curse words being thrown at me right now. I'm not sure these guys will ever look at me as their friend again, and that knowledge stings a bit. The thing is, I'll never tell them that.

We walk up to the house, leaving Vi's shoes and backpack laying in the driveway. The guys take in the view as we step inside. "Nice digs," Lars says.

"It's not mine. It's a rental." One I'll be leaving ASAP, now that it's been found. It actually lasted longer than I expected. I thought for sure I'd only be here a week or two, but then no one was looking for me. Now they're showing up one by one. First Vi, now these guys.

I leave them in the kitchen and go down the short hall to my bedroom and grab the folder that has a yellow sticky note on top of it. Opening it up, I shuffle through the pages."

When I go back to the guys, they're looking around like they're searching for clues. Lars is holding a dirty coffee mug from the sink, likely looking for lip gloss marks. I shake my head. "I thought we were past the fact that Vi was here. What the hell are you looking at?"

Lars sets the mug back in the sink. "Just wondering who else has been here? If you're hiding away with her, there could be other people."

I quirk a brow. "Others? As if there are others that need to hide?"

"Never know with you." Lars rounds the kitchen counter and walks toward me. "Alright, we've seen the folder. Know the story. What do you want done with it?"

I hand Lars the entire folder. "Instructions are on there. Just go to King Corp and leave this on my dad's desk on that date." I jab a finger to the note with a date, two days from now, on it.

Talon grabs the folder from Lars, opens it, looks them over, then waves them in the air. "What's the point of all this shit?"

"It doesn't matter. The point is, I told you to fucking do it."

"Why not just go to him yourself, tell him what you know, and take what you want?" Lars asks, and it's a really good question.

"I want him to tremble. Get a little scared. Start to think of who it is or how he can get out of it. And then I want to take everything from that fucker, and I mean everything." I can feel the unintentional smile grow on my face. I've already contacted an attorney who has a copy of everything. He doesn't know my plan with this evidence, but if things go south, he's permitted to hand everything over to the police.

"If we do this," Talon waves the papers again, "you give us what we want. We end this once and for all."

I smirk. "A deal's a deal."

Lars holds up a finger and takes on a serious tone. "The only reason I'm doing this is because, despite all the deranged things you do, Zed, I trust you. I really fucking shouldn't, but you've never gone back on your word. Don't start now. Don't make us regret this."

I hold my fist out to him, knowing that there's a good chance he'll leave me hanging, but to my surprise, Lars bumps it back. "From start to finish," I tell him.

Talon holds his out, shocking the shit out of me. "Let's finish this shit."

CHAPTER TEN

Pacing the length of the room, lost in thought, I can't help but feel like I'm being played here. It's been two hours since Zed demanded I get out of that tiny town and come into the city.

Here I am—at the hotel he told me to go to. Checked in under his name, and now I'm waiting anxiously in this luxurious suite with the most breathtaking view of the entire city. There's a king-size bed in the main room with a desk and a swivel chair, as well as a small kitchenette at the entrance, and a separate private bedroom with a shared bathroom.

I stop at the open doors that lead onto a large, hooded deck. The sun is setting and the buildings are all aglow from this standpoint. Different colors of neon paint the skylights. There's some lights flashing from emergency vehicles. In the distance, a couple is walking and enjoying each other's company while holding hands. Everything out there is alive; everything in this room is still and quiet.

Hunger pangs in my stomach remind me that I haven't eaten today. Well, the room is under Zed's name. He told me to come here and make myself comfortable. He didn't actually say the words, but what else could he have implied? I step away, leaving the doors open and enjoying the fresh air and the sounds of the busy streets below.

Flopping down on my stomach, I flip open the room service menu and my hungry eyes take it all in. Wanting a little bit of everything.

I decide on the rice pilaf, a salad with no dressing, and apple pie. Once I make the call, I instruct them to leave it inside the door, then I find my way to the bathroom.

Fancy accommodations are nothing new to me, but they aren't exactly part of my everyday life. We traveled a bit when I was a kid, but as life became busier for my parents, we never really left Redwood.

There's a plush white robe with the word *Lunya* engraved above the breast pocket. My fingers rim the hem of the sleeves and I smile. Dinner, comfort, and maybe a glass of that fancy champagne in the wine cooler sounds like a perfect night.

I crank the shower to hot and let the steam fill the room before my clothes drop, layer by layer, into a pile on the floor. While I wait for it to get to just the right temp, I walk naked back into the kitchenette and open and shut cupboards until I find a crystal champagne flute.

I pull open the wine cooler and grab a bottle of Dom Perignon Rosé, then hold my breath and pop the top. The cork flies across the room and I shriek as it smacks right into the sixty-inch flat screen television. No harm done.

Pouring myself a glass, it bubbles up and I sip up the excess before it drips over the brim of the glass, then I take a mouthful. My tongue sweeps lazily across my bottom lip and I carry the glass with me back to the bathroom.

I continue to sip as I walk, then slam it back all at once before setting the glass on the marbled, double-sink vanity in the bathroom. The mirror is completely fogged over and it's my cue that the shower is ready. I've always preferred insanely hot showers.

There's just something about the hot water hitting your bare skin that makes you feel relaxed.

My head dips back and I close my eyes, letting the water trickle down. My nails slither down my body, leaving a trail of goosebumps. I tug my lip ring between my teeth and I bring my head forward, peering down at my body. I don't drink often and the glass of champagne has left behind a burning sensation that simmers through every inch of my body. I suddenly feel daring—out of control and careless.

Bringing one leg up, I rest my foot against the tiled wall and slide a hand down and between my parted lips. With the pad of my index and middle finger, I begin rubbing circles around my clit. Tingles shoot from my touch onward and I roll my hips as I pick up the pace. Who needs a cock when you can give yourself a mind-shattering clitoral orgasm all on your own?

Sliding my fingers up and down in an abrasive, rhythmic motion, the water falls down, coating my hand and only adding to the pleasure I'm bringing myself.

"Ahh," I cry out in a swaddled groan. I hold back, afraid that someone might hear me. Though, the walls in this place are pretty thick and no one is here. Zed is probably miles away. He might even be back in Redwood for all I know.

I keep rubbing and my body fills up with what feels like trapped air, making me lightheaded and leaving my mind in a complete haze. All modesty flies out the window as I rub harder and faster, letting my sounds release out at whatever high-pitched moan escapes me. I don't hold back. "Oh God," I scream in pleasure as I ride my hand and let my orgasm carry me to the peak of an all-time high.

The sensation fades, leaving behind a sensitivity to touch. My nerves feel like they've been zapped by a high voltage of electricity. Even the water dripping down my legs has my thighs clenching. I stand there for what feels like minutes, clearing my head.

My focus shifts from myself and I realize that I never grabbed the wrapped soap off the vanity. Drawing the curtain back, I go to step out, but I freeze when I see two owl-like eyes staring back at me from the corner of the bathroom. He stares right into the shower and I know damn well he watched the entire thing.

The witness to my self-pleasure is wearing a smirk and an erection that raises the fabric of his black sweats. I peel my eyes off it and grab the curtain to shield my body. "What the hell, Zed?" I spit out in a huff.

He begins a slow clap that has my cheeks catching fire. "Well done. Couldn't have done it better myself."

I pull the curtain closed in humiliation and hide behind it. My face drops into my hands. "How long were you here?" I say, loud enough that he can hear me over the running water.

The next thing I know, the curtain is being pulled back and Zed's butt-ass naked body is stepping in front of me. "Get out!" I shout.

"After that, I'm not sure I can. Fuck, Vi. That was sexy as hell."

It takes a lot to embarrass me, to piss me off, or to make me feel inferior, but in a matter of sixty seconds, Zed has done all three.

With wide eyes, I look past him and glue my stare to the shower wall behind him.

Do not look at his gorgeous body. Do not look into his eyes. And most importantly, do not look at his dick.

Fuck. I looked.

I try to look away, but I can't. I take note of the perfect bend that was hitting my G-spot just this morning. His silk head is perfectly shaped and I'd say he's at least a good eight inches. I never remember it looking this big. Then again, aside from this morning, it's been years. It certainly felt big when it was popping my cherry on the bed of his old pickup truck.

"Like what you see?"

I'm finally able to peel my eyes away and look up at him. "Your ego is far too big for that head."

His brows waggle. "Which one?"

I try really hard not to laugh because it will pretty much be giving in to him. He'll think it's acceptable that he stood outside the shower and watched me in a pretty private and vulnerable moment. And now, he stands here naked in front of me like it's no big deal.

My eyelids close slightly and I shake my head. Crossing my arms over my chest, I attempt to cover my breasts, but little good it does. His eyes regard them, making me feel even more exposed than when they were just hanging freely.

"I'm done here," I say before I go to step out.

Before I can, he grabs my arm and pulls me back. My wet body slams against his dry one as the water hasn't even touched his skin yet. His dark and messy hair is looking sexy as ever. His touch feels warm, and his mouth looks delicious. It's been so long since I've looked at Zed this way. I wasn't sure I ever would again. When he was helping me, I never once thought about the way he used to make me feel—the way he's making me feel right now. As if I'm the only girl in the world who matters.

"Don't go."

"Why?" I choke out. My voice sounds gruff and not like my own.

"Because you haven't washed up yet." He opens his palm. Lying in his hand is an opened bar of soap that's melted into a sudsy mess.

I grab the soap from him. Our eye contact not breaking once. I'm not even sure that I've blinked in the last thirty seconds. With both hands, I lather and rub the soap across my stomach, down my arms, and then I do something that surprises us both. I grab his hand and massage the soap up and down his arm. His fingers lace around mine and my breath hitches. Something quills in my chest. Zed's eyes gloss over and it's a new look. A look of astonishment. Did he feel it, too?

No. That's impossible. Zed doesn't have feelings for me. He never has and he never will. To him, I'll always be the girl next door—the one who cried wolf far too many times. I've always been an inconvenience in his life; he's made that perfectly clear.

"Why did you make me leave?" I ask, slicing the tension between us.

I look down and grab his other arm. He doesn't put up a fight. I know it's painful for him to be touched when he's not the one initiating it. I can feel him tense up, but I keep rubbing, leaving behind an abundance of white foam. With his other arm draped at his side, his eyes watch my movements as he speaks. "Someone came. It was time to leave," he says in a frail and soft tone.

Without lifting my head, I peer up at him. Our eyes catching fire again. "Who?"

"Just...someone."

It suddenly feels as if I'm talking to a child who was just caught with his hand in the cookie jar. Zed behaves as if this is the first time he's ever been touched by another person, but I know that not to be true.

My eyebrow lifts. "What's wrong with you?" I ask, being the blunt person that I am.

"What do you mean?" He remains still. Now watching my strokes again. I drop his other arm and wash his stomach, my fingers capering over his six-pack abs.

"You're acting weird. You're the one who just caught me touching myself and you're the one who got in here on your own free will."

A low rumble climbs up his throat. "I'm not acting weird."

His shoulders draw back when I put my soap-filled hand over his heart. I smile up at him. "Your heart's beating fast." It really is. Probably about one hundred beats a minute, if I had to guess.

"What can I say, I'm excited to have a naked girl standing in front of me."

"*A* naked girl? As in any?"

His dick has softened now, so I know it's not arousal. Something else has him acting strange. Before I can put together another thought, his fingers tangle in my soaked hair and our mouths collide.

Zed tips my head to the left and cocks his head to the opposite side. My mouth opens a smidgen, allowing his tongue to sweep in and tangle with mine.

"What—" I go to speak, but he silences me by pressing harder and completely taking my mouth as his own personal hostage. My arms swoop under his and I bring my palms to his back.

There is something so different about this kiss. It's intense and harsh, but more than that, it's passionate. I can feel it in my chest. Grabbing my heart and squeezing it. Threatening to shatter it all over again. I have to stop this. I can't do it again. My hands move to his shoulders and I go to push him away to no avail. "Zed," I say through our welded lips. I push him again, harder this time. "No, Zed. I can't do this."

His head draws back and he looks at me with sadness in his eyes and disappointment in his tone. "Why?"

"Why?" I pique. "Why? Maybe because we've been down this road, and, in your exact words, it's a dead-end."

I tear the shower curtain open and step out. God, I would have loved to give him all of me just now. But this is different than this morning. It was just sex then. It's crazy how sometimes a kiss can mean so much more than sex itself. This time it did. I felt it in my bones and it's scary as hell.

As soon as I grab a towel, Zed grips the curtain and pulls it open farther. The metal loops holding it in place clank together and they all crash into the wall with a thud. "What the fuck, Vi?"

I ignore him and continue to wrap the towel around myself. As soon as I head to open the door, he stops me. Dripping wet, full of dominance. "No. You don't get to just leave me like that."

"Oh?" I quirk. "You want an explanation, do you?" My head rolls in a sassy manner. "How about you give me one first." My tone drops abruptly. "What the hell are you doing, Zed?"

"Forget it." He snatches another towel from the holder and rips the door open himself. Giving me his toned and perfectly shaped ass cheeks as my view. I watch him walk away until he's no longer in sight.

Once he's gone, I close the door gently and let my towel fall to my feet.

It was the right thing to do. I have to protect my heart. Zed can never love me. I don't think he's even capable of allowing himself to love anyone.

CHAPTER ELEVEN

ZED

I shake the towel aggressively against my head, disheveling my hair and hopefully knocking some damn sense into myself.

That was the stupidest fucking thing I've ever done. Letting her see me like that. Standing there mimicking a boy who'd been touched for the first time in his life. I have no idea what came over me. It's that, in that moment, nothing else mattered. It was just us. No dark past, no harrowing memories, not him, not her —just us.

I was mesmerized. Totally fucking captivated by her touch. It's nothing I'd ever felt before. Even back then, it was never that intense. All I know is, I never want to feel it again.

Or maybe I want to feel it over and over again. *What the fuck is wrong with me?*

Letting myself fall under the spell of a chick—pretending that there's this magnetic pull and if I just give in, I could fall in love and live the American dream. The fence, the dog, the kids. I laugh out loud at myself. Yeah, fucking right. Those are not in the cards for me and a life like that doesn't exist, at least not for me.

The bathroom door creaks open and there's a sudden shift in the air when she enters the room. Vi has always carried this confidence and 'I don't give a fuck' attitude that drives me crazy. She also has eyes that drive me wild, and a laugh that would be contagious to anyone who was capable of fully feeling the happiness that it projects.

For some reason, I crave to hear it. Instead, I just look over at her sad face and her slouched posture. "Zed?" she says my name in question.

She comes closer and I rip my attention off of her and jerk up a pair of clean boxer briefs.

Her voice rises. "Why are you so angry all the time?"

Why am I angry? How about because you just molested me in the shower and made me feel something that I don't wanna feel. Only, I don't say it. Not this time.

"I'm not mad that you came into the bathroom. Don't even care that you got in the shower. It's not like—"

"You should be!" I shout, cutting her off. "You should be mad. Stand up for yourself, Vi. Kick my ass out next time." I snatch my shirt off the bed and pull it over my head.

She lets out an airy but sarcastic laugh. "I have no problem standing up for myself when it's necessary. Maybe I just...maybe I wanted you there."

I swallow hard, hold my breath, then exhale deeply. *Don't play into it.* Everything polished and perfect leaves eventually. It's the shallow and soulless who stick around. I should know. I'm not even sure I have a soul. Maybe I just want hers because of that very reason. I could just take it. Take her and force her to stay forever against her will. Pretend that she loves me. Wouldn't be the worst of my sins.

Then again, I tried to fill an empty void in my life at one point and convinced myself that Marni could love me if I tried hard enough—that was a big fucking mistake. It would have never worked, anyway. That void was put there by the girl standing in a robe in front of me. An angel with wings at her side and horns on her head.

The knife in my back is still nuzzled in there tightly, and every once in a while, I can feel it shift as a reminder that we were just temporary. I was just there to fill an empty space for her at a time when she needed me. When she didn't, she turned to Luca. And when Luca left, she had no one but herself, and no one but herself to blame.

"Are you even listening to anything I'm saying to you right now?"

My brows shoot to my forehead. "Huh?" I didn't even realize she was still talking.

She hugs the robe tighter and takes a seat on the foot of the bed. Her damp black hair lays carelessly down her back and her black-painted toes curl into the balls of her feet. "I said I'm sorry for dragging you into this mess."

Did she drag me? I don't think she did. I sweep the air with my hand. "No sense in rehashing shit. What's done is done."

Her head hangs down and her chin presses to her chest. "You always say that."

I step into a clean pair of black sweats and pull them up. "Say what?"

"What's done is done. That's your go-to motto whenever I try to talk about the past."

"Then maybe it's time to quit talking about it." I walk into the small, adjoining kitchen and notice an opened bottle of champagne on the counter. I pick it up and observe it, then set it back down. "Where's the cork?"

"You're deflecting, Zed. Knock that shit off. You know I hate it."

I look around the room and spot it lying next to the wall beneath the mounted television. Small strides lead me over to it.

"Zed!" Vi shouts. "Would you talk to me? Please!"

Breathe in. Breathe out. In one breath, I huff. "What do you wanna talk about?" I pinch my eyes shut and mentally prepare myself for the fact that this will end with Vi in tears.

"You. Me. Us. Hell, I dunno. I'd like to talk about three years ago when we went from best friends to strangers. Or how, after everything, you're still standing here."

"There is no us. Never was."

Her head lifts. Her eyes set on mine. "How can you even say that?"

"How can you pretend there was? Vi." I say her name like it's a sentence all on its own. "We were kids. We fooled around a little bit. Had some fun. It was nothing. We both know that."

She nods slowly and subtly. "Yeah. You're probably right. I guess it was just all in my head."

It wasn't just in your head.

"Good. Now, can we quit talking about this shit?" There's a knock at the door that grabs both our attention. "Who the hell is that?"

Vi springs up and heads toward the door. "I forgot I ordered room service." She pulls the door open and is greeted by a tall and slender guy.

Watching intently, my jaw ticks when the guy skims the length of her body and his lips tug up in a flirtatious smile. "Hey there." His brows waggle and it's only a split second before I'm at her side.

"You can go now. Thanks," I tell our unwanted bellhop. Vi shoots me a perplexed look when I rob him of the tray in his hands.

I go to shut the door, but she protests and grabs it before it closes. "Don't be so rude." Leaving the door wide open and me left in this really awkward position, she walks over to the bed and digs in her bag.

When I look back at the guy, I notice he's looking right at her ass. Even though it's cloaked in a thick robe, it irks me. I scowl deeply, feeling my forehead wrinkle. "You got a problem?" My fists ball at my sides.

"Hmm. No, sir. No problem at all."

Vi takes notice of my stance and swats my arm. "Stop it," she grits through her teeth in a hushed tone.

She hands the guy a ten-dollar bill and finally lets me close the door on him. As I turn around to go back into the deep of the room, I notice the shit-eating grin on Vi's face. "What's with you?" I ask.

Her arms cross over her chest, her smile never faltering. "You were jealous."

"Fuck that. I was not jealous."

"Ohhh, you were very jealous. That guy was checking me out and you didn't like it."

I blow out air and walk past her, ignoring her accusations.

"Come on. Admit it."

Her words echo through my head and my pulse quickens as I lose all patience. I spin around, grab her by the waist and toss her onto the bed. Her legs bend at the knees and I invite myself between them. With leveled eyes, I make my point. "I wasn't jealous. For all that douchebag knew, I was your boyfriend. You're in a robe in a room with a guy. I mean, anyone would think that. Yet, this fucktard comes to the door and flirts with you like I'm not even here."

Her legs cage me in and she responds with a devious little smirk that I wanna bite off her pretty lips. My cock stiffens, eyes skimming her mouth. Her hips buck up, but I won't give in. I refuse to. "You're riding the wrong bus, little girl. Maybe you should go find the bellhop if you're looking for a good time."

She doesn't say anything. Just lies there all too pleased with herself.

"I wasn't jealous," I say for the last time.

Why would I be? Vi is mine, and only mine. She always has been.

CHAPTER TWELVE

This seriously tastes like the best rice pilaf I've ever eaten. I scoop up a pile on my spoon and fill my mouth.

"Good?" Zed asks from the desk chair. His legs are stretched out and his elbow is perched on the arm of the chair while he grazes his thumb over his chin. I didn't even realize he was watching me.

"So good," I say with a mouthful of rice. An idea suddenly comes to me and I climb to my knees on the bed eagerly. "Hey, we should watch *The Outsiders* like old times."

Zed chuckles. "That old movie? Probably isn't available anymore."

"I'm sure we could find it. All these streaming sites now. It has to be on one of them. Come on, it'll be fun."

The chair spins around until he's facing the desk. He grabs a pack of smokes and pulls out a cigarette. When he angles his head toward me, he's got a lighter in his hand and the butt perched between his lips. "Not really in the mood for that shit," he says with the cigarette dangling from his mouth.

"You're no fun anymore." I drop back down on the bed and

pick up my plate of food. Poking and picking, I'm suddenly not hungry anymore.

Zed flips open the Zippo in his hand and a flame stills in front of his face. "People change." He moves the lighter closer and draws in a breath as the cherry on the end of his cigarette comes to life. A cloudy breath of smoke extinguishes the flame of the lighter.

"Yeah, no kidding," I snarl before setting my plate down on the nightstand to my left. "You know you're not supposed to smoke in here." It's a statement, not a question, because, of course, he knows that.

His shoulders rise, then fall. "I'll pay the extra cleaning fee." Dropping his head back, he closes his eyes and raises his hand, taking another drag of his cigarette.

Smoking is the most disgusting habit, but hell if he doesn't make it look sexy. I thought for sure he quit a while ago, but I'm starting to realize there is a lot I don't know about this new Zed. The longer I look at him, the more suffocating the room becomes. I'm not sure how it's possible to miss someone who is sitting right across the room from you, but I do. I miss the old Zed. Even if he was still a sarcastic asshole, at least he talked to me in full sentences and allowed himself to live a little. The guy I'm looking at now is so broken and lost.

There's a bite in my stomach as it begins twisting in knots and a lump lodges in my throat. *I need to get out of this room.*

I get off the bed and scoop up my plate and head toward the door.

"Where the hell are you going?" Zed asks through another cloud of smoke. He gives the butt of his cigarette a flick and the ashes fall onto the cherry oak desk.

I grouse at his carelessness. "I don't know. Somewhere." I pull open the door and step out in my bare feet with the plate balanced in the palm of my right hand.

Once the door closes behind me, I set the plate down on the

floor by the door for housekeeping. Then I take a deep breath and press my back to the wall.

That man makes me crazy. He's the only person who can make me feel a dozen different emotions in a matter of seconds. I can go from missing him, to loving him, then to hating him in the blink of an eye.

Right now, I just don't want to feel. Everything has been so overwhelming lately and for once, I don't even want to think.

My back slides down the wall until I'm on my ass. It's so quiet out here, yet so loud with the thoughts that won't go away.

When did everything go so wrong?

It's only been two days since Luca arrived and I already feel like I've known him forever. He's so relaxed and cool. Confident and comfortable in his skin. I catch myself gawking at him like a lovesick school girl often and have to snap myself out of it. Tomorrow, we'll be starting school at Redwood—him a senior, while I'm just a measly freshman.

Eventually, he'll start hanging out with girls and the thought makes me sick. Even if he is just staying here temporarily while Mom tries to 'fix' him, I want to keep him forever.

It's just a childish crush, Vi, I remind myself for the umpteenth time.

Luca comes in and snatches up a bag of potato chips from my hand. "You know these things are terrible for you, right?"

I go to grab them back, but he holds them in the air and starts reading off the ingredients. "Acrylamide, aspartame, anti-caking agent. Now that just sounds gross." He tosses the bag down on the kitchen table and pulls out a chair to sit down.

I grab it back and smirk. "And potatoes. Which is a vegetable." My brows flutter as I stuff another chip in my mouth. I point to the flask in his breast pocket. "Not like that stuff is any better."

He pulls it out and unscrews the cap. "Actually, it's all-natural. Corn, barley, wheat." He takes a sip.

The way he licks his lips has me licking mine in response. The smooth tip of his tongue gliding over the wet skin. I shake my head a few times to snap out of it. "Excited for school tomorrow?" I ask, stuffing more chips in my mouth.

"Hell no. Starting a new school is never exciting. My advice to you, follow the rules, get good grades, and stay where you're at. Life's too short to plant roots that never grow."

Feeling like there's no better time than the present, I push on what he said earlier—that he came here for Josh. "Hey, what did you mean when you said you came here for Josh? Do you two know each other or something?"

He searches the room in a lazy sweep, looking over his shoulder, then back to me. "Are your parents or Josh home?"

I shake my head, no. "Don't think so."

"I need to tell you something, Vi." Luca's expression drops as he tenses up. He does another search of the room before he leans over the table and whispers, "I did come here for Josh."

My neck cranes and I exhale an exaggerated breath. "But, why?"

"He's dangerous, Vi. Really fucking dangerous."

Chills shimmy down my spine. How does he know this? We all know that Josh is severely bipolar and when he's off his meds, he's terrifying— even when he's on them, he's scary—but, how does Luca know this?

"Josh was my foster brother before your parents adopted him. He did some really messed-up shit, and I'm here to finally get the truth."

My brows hit my forehead. "Your foster brother? So he knows you and knows you're here? Why hasn't he said anything?"

"Oh, he has. To me. He won't tell you guys. You see, I have a twin sister. Her name is Adaline. She also lived at the foster home with us. Adaline fell down a flight of stairs and she's been in a coma for the last six years." His eyes light up, wide and full of hope. "She woke up last month."

Six years ago is when Josh came to live with us. My parents adopted him only months later. I'm so confused right now. "What's this have to do with Josh?"

"She remembered. She told us everything. Josh pushed her down those stairs."

That was the last time I talked to Luca. The next day, he was killed in a car accident off Route 33. Apparently the brakes went out in his car. *Apparently.* I know it was Josh. I saw him go into the garage in the middle of the night. The next day, the cameras were all erased. I never told a soul because I was so scared of what he might do next. A couple months later, I did a search out of boredom, and I found Luca's sister—Adaline. She's a bit rough around the edges and curses more than I do, which says a lot, but she's had such a hard time after Luca's death. We decided to keep in touch, but eventually, we were forced to never speak again for the sake of our secret.

It's so sickening what Josh put my family through. My parents tried so hard to make him feel like he was part of the family. To them, he was. Dad even named his best friend his godfather and they all spent so much time together. But Josh never appreciated anything. He just took us all for granted. I have no regrets about what I did—only that I wish I'd done it sooner.

I push myself off the floor, feeling nauseous as my mind plays these awful memories on repeat. Day in and day out, they're always there.

I go to open the door back up, but it's locked and I don't have the key. My knuckles knock continuously until Zed pulls the door open. "Sorry. Forgot my key," I tell him with a placid tone.

"What's wrong?" he asks.

"Just tired." I walk by him and he closes the door. Everything on my mind and heavy on my heart diminishes. A smile spreads across my face and butterflies wave rapidly through my stomach. "You found it?" I press my lips together and look at Zed.

"Guess it isn't a rarity like I thought." He plays it off like it's no big deal, but to me, it's everything.

I slide on the bed and move until my back hits the headboard. "Watch it with me?" I say to Zed, who's standing in the kitchenette area.

He comes toward me with two full glasses of champagne.

"Nothing better to do in this hellhole." He hands me a glass of champagne and rounds the bed to the other side.

That would be Zed's way of saying, yes. He might not be the best with words, but I can read through his asshole ways. I might be the only person on the planet who understands what he's really saying and is okay with the responses he gives. I know Zed has a heart. I've seen it and felt it. Now I want to mend it.

I take a sip, the smile never leaving my face. Zed sits down on the opposite side of the bed, as far away as he can get. In fact, one leg hangs freely over the side.

"Didn't know you liked champagne," I say to him with my eyes on the television.

I look over at him as he slams the entire glass back. "I don't." He sets it down on the nightstand on his side, then turns to me. "What?"

"Nothing." I take another drink and we watch the movie without saying a word to each other. Once I finish my champagne, I set the empty glass on the table and slither down until I'm lying on my back with my head raised on the pillow.

We're about halfway through the movie when Zed shifts his body until he's all the way on the bed. "You think I've got the same fate as Dally?" he says out of nowhere.

"No," I spit out without any thought behind it. "Absolutely not. Why would you ask that?"

"I dunno. Just forget about it."

I turn on my side to face him. "Tell me why you think that."

"It's just a movie. Forget I said anything."

Zed should know by now that I rarely let things go. "You're gonna be alright, Zed."

His neck pivots slowly until we're looking at one another. "I don't know about that. You will be, though."

A sarcastic breath rides up my airway. "I'm more messed-up than you, and that says a lot. If I'm gonna be okay, there's no doubt you will."

"Nah. You've got friends and a family. You'll be fine."

Where has this boy been? Has he really forgotten everything I've done? "Correction. I have a mom and a dad. I have no friends. Never got close to any girls. You were really the only friend I ever had."

"That's pretty fucking sad if I'm the only friend you've ever had, because I don't even know how to be one of those."

"Sure you do." I tug the blanket up and toss part of it over his legs while the end wraps around my shoulders. "Do you remember when Luca died and you were still so upset with me? Josh went on a rampage. His worst yet. I was walking to my car in tears just because I needed to get out of the house. Didn't even know where I was going. You opened up your bedroom window and hollered my name. You gestured for me to come inside, and I did."

"I also remember you sleeping with no blanket that night because it was cold in my room and I took it."

I laugh at the memory. "Yeah, because I was on your bed and you were on the hard floor. We never said a word to each other that night. But we didn't have to. I always found comfort in the silence with you. As long as you were there, I knew I was safe. You've always protected me, Zed."

"I think you only see what you wanna see."

"And I think you're too hard on yourself." I can tell he's growing bored with this conversation when he slides down and doesn't respond. He rolls on his side with his back to me and doesn't even finish watching the movie.

I give him his space. I've learned that Zed can't be forced into doing anything he doesn't want to do, especially talking. But, like I told him, words aren't always needed.

Twenty minutes later, the credits begin rolling and Zed still hasn't moved an inch. I grab the remote and shut the TV off until we're lying in complete darkness. The only light is the reflection off the buildings that shines through the glass door to the deck. My eyes begin to feel so heavy that I can barely keep them open.

A sudden shift in the mattress has my eyes shooting back open. In front of me, Zed is on his side with his eyes beaming into mine. I can barely make them out, but they glow in the soft light from the door.

We just lie there, looking at one another, without saying anything. It's not awkward or uncomfortable. It's as perfect as a moment can get.

Underneath the blanket, Zed takes my hand and curls two fingers around it. I smile inwardly as my heart doubles in size. My eyes close again and I think I might finally get a good night's sleep.

∞

I WAKE up to the burning hot sunshine beaming into the room. Blinking a few times, I adjust to the light and once I do, I forget for a moment where I'm at. Then it all hits me. Zed was lying here with me. I pat around at the space where he was, but he's gone. I immediately jump out of bed, thinking the worst.

It's ten o'clock in the morning, which is later than I ever sleep. "Zed," I call out quietly.

I notice that the private bedroom door is closed. He must have woken up in the middle of the night and went in there to sleep.

I'm making my way to the bathroom to get cleaned up when I hear voices coming from the bedroom. Only, it's one voice from a two-sided conversation. Unless Zed is now bartering with ghosts.

My ear presses gently to the closed door, and I hold my breath, taking care not to make a sound.

"I scratch your back, you scratch mine. Isn't that how it's

always been?" Zed says to the person on the other end of the call. "No, fuck that, Tommy."

My eyes widen and my heart begins pounding in my chest. *What is he doing?* All it takes is one call and our whereabouts will be known. I keep listening in hopes of finding out where this conversation is going.

"You guys do what I asked and then I'll give you what you want."

I step away slowly. Nausea pools in my stomach and I try really hard not to let this hurt as much as my heart wants it to.

CHAPTER THIRTEEN

ZED

Why does it always have to be a favor for a favor? Whoever came up with that idea is an imbecile. Whatever happened to just helping out a friend with no strings attached? Guess it's pretty hypocritical of me to even expect that.

Regardless, I'll give them what they want. The answers they've been searching for, for months. It's not really a favor to them, but more so, a favor to myself. I've spent months covering my tracks —helping them and sinking myself. I won't let it all be for nothing.

The first letter gets delivered tomorrow. Time to toy with that bastard father of mine for a bit before I set his world on fire. I plan to burn every bad memory that he's catalyzed. In doing so, I'll get myself set for life with what should have never been his in the first place.

There's some rustling in the bathroom that is joined to this private bedroom. I go to open the door, but it's locked. Vi must be awake.

I haven't slept yet, and don't feel tired at all. I laid there watching her sleep peacefully for most of the night and realized that if I didn't get out of that bed, I'd never sleep. Little good it did because I came in here and laid down about two hours ago and her face was still sitting fresh in my head. My thoughts just kept coming back to her. Wondering if this is all worth it. Thinking about how much of a risk I'll be taking.

My head jerks toward the closed bathroom door when there's a loud thud coming from inside. "Vi?" I say, turning the handle again to no avail. "What the hell are you doing in there?"

Another slam.

I head out of the room and over to the other entrance to the bathroom, but that door is locked as well. I knock my knuckles to it. "Open the door."

There's more stirring in the room and a couple smaller thuds before the door opens. Vi is standing there with a fractured smile on her face. "Good morning, Zed." She steps past me.

I follow behind her and she slides her shoes on. "What's up with you this morning?"

"Just going down to the lobby for a coffee. Want one?"

"Nah, I'm good."

She walks away, leaving it at that.

Once I get a glass of water and slam it back, I walk over to the doors that lead to the porch and pull them open. The sun is shining bright and it's dry as fuck out here. Leaning over the railing, something catches my eye. *Fuck.* I cup my hands around my mouth and shout, "Vi!"

"Damnit, what the hell is she doing?" I mumble. Hurriedly, I go back inside and rip open the door to the hallway, then haul ass to the elevator. Tapping the button repeatedly until the damn thing finally stops and the doors slide open.

There's no way I'll get to her in time. Whose car was that? And where is she going?

The elevator moves at an insanely slow speed, then again, it could just be because I'm in a hurry and nothing ever goes my way. I pull my phone out of the back pocket of my jeans and try to call her, but it goes straight to voicemail. Shouldn't be surprised. She's had her phone off the majority of her stay with me.

It finally comes to a stop and I jog through the lobby and out the front doors. But I'm too late. She's gone.

Spotting the receptionist to my left, I go over to her. "There was a girl, about five-foot-three, hundred and ten pounds." I use my hands as a description, leveling her height with my chest. "Do you know where she was going?"

"No, sorry," the receptionist says.

"Fuck!" I shout. My fingers rake through my hair and sweat rims my hairline. The receptionist takes a step back, looking at me like I'm a detonated bomb.

There's an empty couch beside me that I drop down onto. It's probably been sat on by a million different, germ-infested strangers, and I don't even care.

She was so close. I had her right where I wanted her. Not just for the guys, but for myself. For the first time ever, I considered giving her the piece of me she'd always wanted. Now, she doesn't even want it anymore. It's probably better this way. I would have eventually fucked things up and lost her forever, anyway.

Better to just let her go now than try and force her to stay later. The only problem is, I can't protect her when she's gone.

∞

NEVER THOUGHT I'd be coming back to this town because I wanted to. Not that I really want to, but I have to be here for now. Once the pact is done and sealed and we can all move on from this whole Josh mess, I'll probably head somewhere east.

The welcome sign greets me with a big fat, 'ha, you're back' and I flip it off. I've got myself a room at the one and only hotel in this town—or inn, rather. There's no way in hell I'm going back to my dad's house. Normally I'd go crash at Talon's, but I'm beyond the point of rubbing shit in their faces and doing what I want just because I can. Last time I stayed there, I knew I wasn't wanted, but he needed my help and didn't have much of a choice but to let me. I could do it again, but is it really worth it? Do I really want to stay somewhere that I'm not wanted?

Guess if that were the case, I wouldn't even be in this state, this country—heck, even this world. If I were gone, no one would notice. Everyone would carry on with their lives and they'd all be better off without me. I come up to the East Street Bridge and the thought of driving right over the edge crosses my mind. I could end it all right now. No one is here to stop me this time.

Then she flashes in my mind. Maybe she'd care. I think she might be the only person who would.

I take the curve and push those thoughts away. They're harrowing and never-ending and I fear that one day I'll just do it on impulse. The fact that I fear it is slightly reassuring. It means that I must have some will left to live.

Once I'm parked in the hotel parking lot, I try Vi's phone one more time, but it still goes straight to her voicemail. At least she's smart enough to leave it off.

My feet hit the pavement and I slam my door shut behind me, slide my sunglasses up to my forehead, and take a deep breath of the dry and tainted Redwood air.

"Zed?" someone hollers my name. I look to my right and see the chick with the hose from Dad's house jogging toward me. "Hey there." She places a hand on my arm and I look down at it with a scowl.

I shake her hand off of me and slide my shades back down. "What the hell do you want?"

"Wow. I can see you got your dad's sour attitude as well as his good looks."

I immediately notice the marks on her neck, but don't say anything. "Did you need something? I've got shit to do and you're wasting my time."

She steps closer, her breasts intentionally hitting the side of my arm. "Thought maybe you'd like to see what your dad's been getting and you've been missing." She bites her lip, but it's not sexy in the least bit.

"I'm good. Not really into the old man's leftovers."

"It's a shame, really. I've got some moves that would drive you wild." She leans so close that I can smell onion on her breath and it's repulsive.

I brush her off again. "I'm sure you do. Now, go show someone else. I'm not interested." My feet keep moving, but the damn girl doesn't take a hint.

"Okay. Okay, I get it," she says. "Listen, I'm hard up for cash. Your dad kicked me out and I've got nowhere to go. I just need to get a room for the night."

I stop. Then turn around and look at her. I tip my shades and observe the bruises on her neck that run down her shirt. Pulling back the spaghetti strap of her tank top, I notice that they don't end. "Did he do that to you?"

"I...I umm. Don't tell him, please. He'll be so mad at me."

Still watching her with a deep glare, I reach into the back pocket of my jeans and pull out my wallet. "Don't go back there. If you do, you're asking for trouble." I slap a couple Benjamins in her hand and without another word, I go in the main doors of the hotel.

He really is a rotten piece of shit.

Once I'm all checked in, I drop my shit in the room and leave. I might not be staying at Talon's, but that doesn't mean I don't plan on paying them all a little visit. There's been a slight change in plans and I need more from them. I think they'll be inclined to help me with this one, and for the first time, I get to play the 'no questions asked' card.

Mrs. Mayberry, the inn's owner, is still standing at the desk when I go to walk out. She doesn't say a word to me. Didn't when I checked in, either. I'm pretty sure she hates me. Don't blame her, really. I think I was sixteen years old when I stole all her lawn ornaments and put them on display in front of the high school. She had it coming. Who in the world owns thirty-five fucking gnomes? And a couple naked ones at that. Penis and all. It's mind-boggling. I'm actually surprised I didn't think of the grand scheme years before that.

Needless to say, I was busted and had to return them all. Owed her thirty bucks for breaking the head off one she claims was an antique. It was a good laugh, though, and I've got no regrets.

Pushing the door open, the bell jingles until it closes behind me. I get in my truck and head straight for Talon's house. "Hard-wired" by Metallica blasts through the speakers, but it's not enough to silence the thoughts in my head. It's like my mind won't give me a fucking break. Ever since Vi showed up, it's like she's moved permanently into my head.

I just can't understand why she left like that without a word. It seemed like we had a decent night together. I was on my best behavior, didn't insult her at all, didn't yell. She's out there some-where and she could be found at any moment. I've just gotta keep the guys busy, so they don't have time to search.

Maybe she went home? The thought of going to her house crosses my mind, but her snooty bitch of a mother is the last person I feel like seeing. Another lady who doesn't like me. Then again, I know the secrets of her house and I'm pretty sure she's aware of that fact. She knew Vi would come over at night, especially when Josh was at his worst. Vi went to her with her suspicions about Luca's death and her mom just swept it all away, because she wasn't about to have her family name slandered. No, she'd rather let that deranged boy rule her house with an iron fist and torture her daughter.

Nah, there's no way Vi went home.

I glance in the rearview mirror, thinking I see her car, but it wasn't even remotely similar.

Another passes and my heart jumps into my throat—not her.

My hand slaps to my forehead repeatedly. "Get the fuck out!"

I turn down Talon's road, then whip into his driveway and slam on the brakes.

Just fucking great. Everyone's here. As per usual, the driveway is lined with familiar cars. Lars, Marni, Tommy, even Wyatt with his neon pink hubs.

Don't these kids go to school anymore? I look at the clock on the dash that reads four-thirty. Guess school's out for the day.

My feet hit the pavement and I walk up and in the house like it's perfectly normal for me to barge right in. I'm not sure that I've ever knocked on this door, and I probably never will. When the time comes that I think I have to, I won't come here anymore. Not because I feel entitled, but because it will mean that these friendships have completely dissolved.

As soon as I walk in, I blister at the unwanted glances. Feeling like the huge-ass outsider that I am. The laughter and voices stop, everyone just looks at me, waiting for me to move, to speak, to do something.

Casually, I walk over to the couch and drop down in the only empty space—right next to Marni. Her legs are tucked in like a pretzel and my outer leg accidentally bumps her knee, causing her to move it with a nasty snarl.

"How's it going, Little Thorn?" I say to her, expecting a sarcastic response, or at the very least, an eye roll.

She just sits there, completely ignoring me. As if I'm not even in the room. Talon's jaw ticks in a fury as he pulls Marni under his arm. His eyes set on mine, much like everyone else in the room.

Talon finally breaks the silence. "You plan on telling us why the hell you're here when we just found you in Nanjunction only yesterday?"

I throw my hands up, then let them fall in my lap. "What's the point in staying away when people keep popping up everywhere I go?"

Leaning forward, I get a better look at Lars, then Tommy, then Wyatt, who are all just watching me sit here. "Well, boys, it seems as though I'm gonna need that party, after all."

That sure as hell does it. Everyone starts shifting, huffing, puffing, scrambling. Tommy gets to his feet. "Hold up, you told us that all we had to do was deliver some papers. No party, no bodies—just a simple mail delivery."

"You know how it goes. The creative juices get flowing and you realize that your plan just isn't enough. You should know, Tommy. Wasn't your original plan to kidnap the guy holding your hand right now?"

Seems I've hit a nerve. Tommy tosses Wyatt's hand aside and gets to his feet. "You've got some nerve." He points a finger at me and doesn't realize that three are pointing back at him.

Getting fed up with the indignation, I jump to my feet, too. Looking around at all these assholes who sit here and act like I'm the only one who's ever fucked up.

"Fuck you, guys," I shout. I point to Talon. "Fuck you for turning on me because your girlfriend here never once told me to stop. You sit there and turn your nose up at me when you did the same damn thing to her. Need I remind you of the recordings?" I sweep the air with my hand, calling him a lost cause. "You killed your own fucking father."

I look at Lars. "And fuck you! You held this girl at gunpoint, but everyone loves you because you never actually touched her. What a crock of shit." I blow out air before looking back at Tommy, who's standing there waiting for his turn.

"And you," I point and shake my finger with an airy laugh, "you fucking tied a guy to a chair and tortured him. Pulled out fingernails and all, and who was there to help you? Who never told a single fucking soul because you asked me not to? Me!" I slap my hands to my chest. "I helped you. I helped you all." I flip them all my middle finger and wave it around the room. "Fuck all of you."

There's so much more I could say to each one of them. Like the time that I sucker-punched Billy Winters for grabbing Talon's sister's ass and laughing about it.

Or the time that Tommy called me up when we were freshmen because he thought it sounded like someone was breaking into his house. I went straight there and stood guard all night. Never once called him a pussy.

Then there was the time that Lars was really fucking sick and I asked my mom to make her famous homemade soup because he didn't have a mom to do it for him.

I could remind them of all the times I wasn't the asshole they view me as now, but I don't. You can do a thousand acts of kindness, but fuck-up once and they'll only remember that one fuck up over everything else.

I jump over the couch and head for the door, done with this shit. Done with them.

My hand grabs the doorknob and I give it a pull. "Zed," Marni hollers. "Wait."

I freeze in place, gripping the handle tightly while my hand sweats profusely. After a brief pause, I pull it open and walk out, not caring what anyone has to say right now.

CHAPTER FOURTEEN

Vi

It's only been one month since I left, but coming back to this house feels like I could stay away forever and not miss it one bit.

The scent alone carries so many dark memories that smack me in the face all at once. "In here," Mom hollers from the sitting room.

I don't even bother taking my shoes off. I won't be staying long. Mom called twice today threatening to cancel my cards and phone if I didn't come home and handle things for school. I'm not sure when she started caring so much, but I can't help but wonder why she does.

"Hey, Mom," I say casually, like she's a friend I came to have morning coffee with.

She sets her e-reader down beside her, uncrosses her legs, and pulls off her reading glasses. Still looking as young and proper as she has since I was a kid. One look at me and her mother-stare returns with a vengeance. "Your books and assignments are on the kitchen table. Laptop is in your room. I expect all your work to be completed by the end of the semester."

Turning to walk away, I mumble under my breath, "Good to see you, too."

One month. I've been gone an entire month and she greets me in the same manner she'd greet the mailman when he comes to pick up a package.

The rich kids in this town might have a lot of problems, but outsiders often forget the way we are raised. Lack of love and affection can lead even a saint into darkness.

I go into the kitchen and scoop up the stack of books that are topped with about fifty sheets of paper. It'll take me at least a month just to look through all of this. How in the hell am I supposed to get all this work done in two months? I sigh heavily, then carry the books up to my room to pack a few more things.

Mom gave the okay for me to leave again. Not that she could really stop me. Even if she threatened to take everything away, I'd still leave. There is just no way I can stay in this town, feeling like everyone is breathing down my neck. I might be tough, but my conscience gets the best of me when I'm forced to lie. Not to mention, there are so many people here who are suspicious and most of whom can't stand me. Don't really blame them. I did what I had to do to protect myself, even if it was at the expense of others.

Trying to spend as little time in my room as possible, I pack up a bag and head back downstairs. Mom's waiting at the bottom of the steps, tirelessly. As if she's been waiting there this entire time. "You'll call when you get to Lisa's?" she asks, in a surprisingly mellow tone.

I give her a side-eye and raise a brow. "It's Aunt Lisa. And, sure. If you want me to."

My mom and her sister aren't exactly close. Mom is a lot to handle with her mood swings and lavish lifestyle. Aunt Lisa is very down-to-earth and works as a blackjack dealer in Vegas. Mom collects money; Aunt Lisa counts it. To say they butt heads is an understatement.

"I'd like to know you made it safe. Vegas is a long drive, Vienna."

Who is this lady and where is the one who was just sitting on the couch moments ago?

"It's a couple hours. I've driven farther." When she gives me a pleading look, I give in. "Okay. I'll call. Promise." I take a few more steps down and she begins giving me an awkward look. "What?"

Once I'm at the bottom step, she swoops my hair out from the crease between my neck and shoulder. "What in God's name is that?"

I slap a hand over my neck, remembering that Zed left a massive hickey there the other night. "It's um…a bug bite." I shrug, keeping my cool.

"It'd have to be a mosquito the size of a large cat to leave a mark like that." She goes to move my hand, but I keep it in place. "Are you still on your birth control, Vienna?"

My cheeks ignite in embarrassment. Mom has never once had a talk with me about sex, birth control, or even boys for that matter, so the subject is highly uncomfortable. "How'd you know I was on birth control?"

I wasn't even aware she knew. I got on it after I lost my virginity, thinking that I'd end up becoming the town slut because it felt so damn good. But I never met another guy who was worthy, so I've pretty much been on it for no reason—until now. Well, now it'll probably be another three years because it certainly won't be Zed next time.

"Our insurance pays for it. I do pay attention to things."

I'm surprised by her comment. Here I thought that Mom didn't know anything about me because she didn't care to. "Well, I am on it. And I don't need it. Just so you're aware, I'm not out whoring around."

"Good. Just be careful. There are so many diseases out there and the male species, in general, is the biggest one. They can hurt you more than any blister or itch."

"Oh my God, Mom." I bury my face in my hands as my head shakes. "I can't believe you just said that."

A hand sets on my shoulder. My head lifts, my hands dropping, as I look at her. Suddenly, there is something warm about my mom. A feeling I haven't felt since before Josh moved in. Is it possible that she, too, is finally feeling free of the chains?

There's no doubt that she's still stern and stubborn, but she seems…happier.

"It's true. All men are carriers. It takes the right woman to stop the spread."

Laughter escapes me. My mom actually just made me laugh.

I shoot a thumb over my shoulder. "I should go." I have to get out of here while things are good. Leaving with the memory of my mom making a joke is probably the best way to go out.

"You don't have to go, you know. I know you miss Josh—"

"Wait," I cut her off, wrinkling my nose. "Is that why you think I'm leaving? Mom, I don't miss Josh. Not even a little bit, and for you to even think that I do goes to show that you really did dismiss his behavior all this time." It was never a question if she noticed. Of course she did. But she and Dad both played it off like he was just lost and had a rough upbringing. No! You can have a rough upbringing and still treat others with human decency. Josh was an entitled psychopath.

"I just…you two were always so close."

"No," I stammer. "No, we weren't. Josh made this house feel like hell. He brought out the worst in all of us. How can you even stand there and pretend that he was this golden child?" I throw my hands up. "You really are delusional." Spinning on my heels, I head for the door. So much for parting with a decent goodbye.

"I know," she says, grabbing my attention and causing my movements to freeze.

"What?" I look over at her with my hand wrapped around the door handle.

"I said, I know. Josh definitely made life difficult for all of us." She takes a step back and sits down on the bottom step. "There's just so much you don't understand, Vi. I had to keep loving him. No matter what he did. He's my son."

"But, he wasn't, Mom. Josh was a full-grown child when you adopted him. He came into this house a monster, and he left the same way."

"It was never his fault. It was his reckless mother's. She's the one to blame. Because of her abandonment, he grew up in these homes and witnessed things no child should have to. No one could come out of that kind of madness with a smile on their face."

I did. Mom has no idea what I've been through, and she never will. No one will ever know. I might burn for the things I've done, but it's better than others having to live in hell their entire lives.

"None of it matters. He's gone. But no, I don't miss him. In fact, I'm glad he's gone." I pull the door open and walk out. My heart racing, palms sweating, and everything I've pushed away hits me smack dab in the face as soon as I step outside.

I pull the door closed behind me, and face what's standing right in front of me. "Hi, Willa," I say with a forced smile on my face. With my heavy as hell backpack thrown over one shoulder, I put a hand on my hip. "What are you doing here?"

Willa places one hand on her ginormous stomach, rubbing it gently up and down. "Saw your car in the driveway. I wish I could say I'm surprised to see you back in Redwood, but that would be a lie. I knew you'd come back eventually."

I'm pretty sure my hammering heart is apparent through the fabric of my black tee. I let my bag slide off my arm, unable to hold the weight any longer. "Who else knows I'm here?"

"Just me. For now."

I nod in response, but remain quiet, letting her voice what she has to say. I have to play my cards right or this place will be swarming with Rebels in two seconds flat. After all, she's one of them now. "How dare you?" she spits out, surprising me. It's not like Willa to be confrontational and while I didn't expect this to be pleasant, I didn't anticipate that.

"Excuse me?" I snarl, playing dumb.

"You had the nerve to go on live news and tell the entire world that you think I ran off with your brother when this entire time, you're probably the one who killed him. If I weren't pregnant, I'd probably slap you right now."

The fact that she says it and doesn't do it shows that she's the same Willa Mack. "You wanna slap me, go for it, honey. You're right. I deserve it. But it's not for reasons you think. I really thought you ran off with him. I just did some simple math. How was I to know that you were carrying Lars' baby?"

Her forehead wrinkles in an array of lines as she glares at me. "You wouldn't because it wasn't any of your business."

"You're right. It wasn't. Now, if you don't mind, I have a long ride ahead of me. You can tell your posse, including Zed, that they don't have to worry. They'll never see me again."

"You do realize that running away makes you look even more guilty. If you're innocent, why not stick around and say your piece?"

"I don't owe you or anyone else an explanation for anything I do. Just like your business isn't mine—mine isn't yours."

"Did ya do it?" she deadpans.

Did I do it? That question can pertain to many things, so I'll go with the easiest answer for the unlikeliest of questions. "No, I didn't."

I grab my bag off the ground and throw it back over my shoulder. "I've really gotta go. I wish you the best, Willa."

"I can't keep this from Lars. But I'll give you thirty minutes. I hope you find the escape you need. Just remember, your past is never as far away as you'd like it to be."

"I'll take whatever I can get." I look down at her hand as she rubs her belly again. "I heard it's a girl."

"Yeah. Little Alessi. It means defender in Greek, and Lars is determined to raise her as such." She chuckles, and suddenly, she's the same sweet Willa that I remember.

"I'm sorry I missed the shower. Just have a lot going on. Ya know?"

"Not really. You've never really told anyone anything."

"I never intended to hurt anyone." In fact, it was just the opposite. But I don't say that.

"These guys will never give up until they have all the answers. To be honest, I prefer it happens soon, so we can all move on with our lives. So from the bottom of my heart, I'm asking you to come forward if you know anything at all. For me. For the future of my new family."

I wish I could, but I can't. There's just no possible way.

I walk past her toward my car, and she doesn't stop me. Instead, she walks beside me, until we go our separate ways. She gets in her car, and I get in mine.

Willa is a good person, and I have no ill feelings toward her. Hell, I have no ill feelings toward any of them. I can't stay, though. It's time for me to move on and put the past where it belongs. Even if it will always be there, my past is not my future.

CHAPTER FIFTEEN

ZED

Instead of going back to the hotel, I take a drive somewhere that has great significance in my life. Before everything went to shit, this place was where all the fun happened. There were bonfires, parties, chicks, and beer. We'd kick back and chill without a care in the world.

Occasionally, we'd even bring random girls here, give them a tour in the dark and scare the shit out of them. I smile at the memories as I sit in my truck in front of Briarwood.

I'd like to think it was the night Josh died that everything changed, but truthfully, it was long before that. At least for me, anyway. If I had to pinpoint the exact day that my life started to unravel, it would be the day that I saw Vi kiss Luca. It was the first time I'd ever felt pain so deep that it literally took my breath away. I agonized over it for days. Made it into this big thing in my head until I started believing it myself. I was convinced that Vi no longer needed me. I was the only friend she had in Redwood, and I never told her this, but she was the best friend I ever had.

Maybe I should have just told her that. Words have never been my strong suit. I don't like emotions, in fact, they downright freak me out. Telling people how you feel makes you vulnerable. It opens the doors for more pain and that's the last thing I need.

After that day, Mom slowly got sicker. Then she passed away. I'd lost the only two people I'd ever loved and it felt as if I had nothing left to fight for.

The Bluetooth rings through while my phone flops around on vibrate in the passenger seat.

Lars' name flashes on the screen.

I contemplate ignoring it, because I don't think we have anything more to say to one another, but on a whim, I decide to answer.

Once I tap *Accept* on the screen, I don't say anything. If he's got something to say, he can say it.

"Hello. You there, Zed?"

"What do you want?"

"We all talked after you left. Tell us where you want the party and we'll make it happen."

I'm not surprised. I knew they'd do it. Why wouldn't they? They want something from me. "Glad you changed your mind."

"When and where?"

I lean back in the seat, stretch my legs out, and take in the view of the place that's loaded with memories—why not make some more? "Saturday. At Briarwood."

"Why Briarwood?"

"Why not?"

There's a long pause and some shuffling. Pretty sure he's holding his hand over the phone and getting approval from Talon.

"Alright. Anything else we need to know?"

"I'll be there around eight o'clock to make my appearance. That's all you need to know."

"Alright. Guess we'll see you then. Oh, and you can thank Marni for this. She's the one who voiced that she thinks we should help you."

Marni? That doesn't make sense. She hates me more than any of them.

"Hey," I say, stopping him from ending the call, "I still need those papers delivered. It has to happen before Saturday. Tell everyone to stick to the schedule I gave them."

"And in return, we get what...hold on a sec." His hand goes over the phone again, but I can still hear him, though it's hard to make out the words. "It's Zed. You what?"

There's some shuffling and a long pause before he returns to the line. "Well, well, well," he tsks. "It seems that Vi Moran isn't as far away as we thought."

"What the hell is that supposed to mean?"

"Willa ran into Vi. Apparently she's leaving the state. But you probably know this already, don't you? You planning on going with her?"

My entire body flies forward and I shift into drive, without even putting on my seatbelt. I completely ignore his questions. "Willa saw Vi? Where?"

"Her house. Guess she saw her car and—"

I don't even listen to the rest of whatever he has to say. I peel out of the driveway and head straight for Vi's.

Leaving the state? What the fuck is this girl up to?

I'm doing seventy in a fifty-five, hauling ass when I come into town. I don't even slow down. A simple tap of the brakes at a stop sign, and I fly down the road toward Vi's street—my street.

I make the seven-minute drive in four minutes and whip into Vi's driveway. At the same time, another car pulls in behind me. Lars.

All three guys hop out and shut their doors simultaneously. I don't even bother getting out. They all swarm my truck at the same time, but I just sit there, waiting patiently for whatever is coming my way.

"Where'd she go?" Talon asks. When my only response is a sly sneer, he reaches in the open window and grabs me by the collar of my tee shirt. "Tell us, damnit."

Laughter climbs up my throat. "You think I'd be sitting in her fucking driveway if I knew where she was?"

"Fine," he titters, "you don't wanna tell us what you know. I'll ask her mom." He gives me a shove, then releases his grip on me.

Before he can even take a step, I swing my door open, hitting him in the side of his leg. I've had just about enough of his shit. In the same manner he used, I grab him. My fingers clench around his shirt and I slam his back against the back door of my truck. I shout, "Do you have any idea how fucking sick I am of your mouth?"

"Get off him," Marni hollers as she comes running up to us. Willa wobbles behind, but I pay them no attention.

I'm tired, I'm cranky, and I'm really fed up with this shit. "Move on with your fucking lives," I shout louder, gripping him tighter. His arms flail and hit me a couple times, but I don't even care. "What the hell happened to you? I don't even fucking know you anymore."

Marni shuffles toward us, but Tommy puts an arm out, stopping her from intervening. "This needs to happen."

Lars and Tommy stand by idly, and I'm pretty impressed because they're always front and center, ready to break this shit up.

"So you guys are just gonna let them fight? Are you crazy?" Marni squalls in a high-pitched tone that rings through my ears.

Talon quits fighting back, so I loosen my grip but still keep a hold on him. "Life fucking happened. That's what."

"You think you're the only one with a shitty upbringing? Nightmares that never stop? And a weight on your shoulders that pushes you down, day in and day out?" Heat rises to my face, an anger so formidable that if he says one wrong thing, I might not be able to control myself. "You've got a fucking sister who loves you. Enough money to buy yourself a fucking continent. You've got the girl of your dreams, and you've got friends that would do damn near anything for you. Don't stand there and act like your life's in shambles."

Talon grits through his clenched teeth, "You've got two seconds to back up before I headbutt you and knock your damn teeth out." He goes to make a move, but I jam my knee into his thigh and dig until he stops squirming. He's bigger than me, but my adrenaline won't let him win.

"You think I fucking care? You think that pain will weaken me? I don't give a damn what you do to me. Three days ago I was ready to jump off a fucking cliff because I hate myself so much. You can't touch me, Talon. None of you fucking can."

My hands drop, I take a step back and realize they're all looking at me with pity. Or hatred. I can't really tell the difference. I should have just kept my mouth shut, but I'm not sure I can anymore. If I don't do this now, I might actually make it over the ledge next time.

Tommy comes forward and goes to place a hand on my shoulder, but I slap it away. "Don't fucking touch me." I take another step back.

"I had no idea," Lars says, with a sadness in his eyes that I've seen before. It's the same look he had when he told me his mom left. That night I stole a six-pack of beer from the grocery store downtown and we got our first real buzz.

I sweep the air with my hand, then pull open the door to my truck that somehow got closed. "Doesn't matter. Get your car outta my way," I tell Lars, who has his vehicle parked bumper to bumper to mine. Pretty sure he did that so I couldn't get out. But I'll ram his car with my truck and push it back if I have to.

When he doesn't move, I shout, "Now, damnit."

His hands fly up. "Alright, man. I'll move it."

I point from Talon to Tommy. "Stay the hell away from me. And if any of you go near Vi, you'll live to regret it."

They all share a look as if I just said something surprising.

"I saw Vi today," Willa chimes in for the first time this evening.

I don't respond because I don't wanna hurt the pregnant girl's feelings. Instead, I just ignore her. I already know she saw Vi. Lars told me so.

"She mentioned she was leaving the state? Did you know that?"

Stop talking, damnit.

Lars' car backs up and pulls off to the side of the road, giving me a clear shot out of here.

I climb in my truck and go to shut the door, but mid-shut, Vi's front door opens. Her mom steps outside with a perplexed look on her face. "What in the world is going on out here? You do realize that there are cameras watching you? If you plan on stealing something, you *will* get caught."

Everyone goes quiet. I need these guys to get the hell out of here without engaging in conversation with Vi's mom. "Tommy, get them all out of here before Mrs. Moran calls the cops."

"Come on, guys. We can touch base with Zed later about the party."

I give him a nod of appreciation, right before Lars starts approaching the front of the house. "What the hell are you doing?" I holler to him.

"Just going to have a word with Vi's mom," he retorts with sarcasm.

"Come on, Lars, just let this go," Willa shouts to him.

Tommy jogs the couple feet up to him. "Yeah, let's get outta here."

When he doesn't stop, I get back out of the truck, leaving my door open. I bypass Lars and go straight for the front porch. Vi's mom shoots daggers at me and her lip curls more and more with each step I take. "Hey, Mrs. Moran. Why don't you go inside and I'll get these guys outta here," I tell her in a calm and collective tone.

I'm too late, because she's still standing there, examining us like we're a puzzle spread out on her porch, when Lars comes to my side.

"If anything, they need to get you out of here. You're the worst of them all," she scoffs. "Sneaking my daughter in your house in the middle of the night when she was only fifteen years old. Then breaking her heart, and now what, you're trying to do it all over again. You're the reason she's leaving me, aren't you?"

I'm at a loss for words. Completely fucking shocked, humiliated, ashamed. And more than that, really confused how she knows all this. She caught Vi at my house a few times, but after a while, she just stopped trying to catch her and let her stay. Mrs. Moran knew what Vi was scared of because she was scared of the same thing.

"What is she talking about?" Lars asks, looking at me in astonishment.

"Nothing." I grab him by the back of the shirt and start pulling him away. "Just ignore her. She's still grieving Josh."

I continue to pull Lars back while the others stand in the driveway watching. Before we get to them, he jerks away, but stands directly in front of me. "Is what she said true?"

I'm not sure why I feel like everything still needs to be a secret, but I do. I guess I always just thought that if we were seen together and Vi eventually came out about what happened, I'd be associated with it. It was my biggest fear. I never wanted those nightmares to see the light of day. Now, I have no reason to keep it a secret. But, I still feel like I need to. If people know about me and Vi, they'll try and break us. What we have is special and untouchable—even if it is completely fucked-up—it's ours. It's *our* secret.

"Yeah. It's true. So what? Vi and I have a past. Doesn't mean shit."

Damnit, I wish I knew how to talk normal to people. It's like my mind thinks this shit up, but my mouth doesn't let me say it. I could tell him that Vi is the only person alive that I would die for, that I've loved her since the first time I saw her catching fireflies in her back yard. Or that I saved her life and she saved mine.

But, I don't. Because I don't know how. My thoughts get muddled, my heart races. I guess I just worry that if I let people in, they'll leave.

"Alright. Well, that's cool. I guess." His shoulders shrug and he walks back to the guys, not saying another word about it.

With my hands in my pockets, I stand by my truck, waiting for them to leave first. Hopefully this means that they'll stay away from Vi's house now. Not that it matters, she's gone and I don't think she's coming back.

Everyone piles into Lars' car, but before he gets in, he stands on the door frame and slaps his hand on the roof. "Party next Saturday at Briarwood. See ya there." He does a subtle wave and drops down, shuts his door, and takes off.

The party, my act, and everything else is the furthest thing from my mind. I need to find Vi, and I think I know where to start.

I slam the door to my truck closed and head back up to the front door of the house.

Taking a deep breath, I press the doorbell, then exhale slowly.

The door flies open and I'm greeted, once again, with devil eyes and a death glare. "I thought I told you—"

I hold up a hand, stopping her. "Can I just have a minute?" I haven't used this word in years, "Please?"

Mrs. Moran steps aside and waves a hand to allow me in, the scowl never leaving her face. "Make it quick."

CHAPTER SIXTEEN

I'm only twenty minutes into the drive, after stopping for gas just outside of Redwood and hitting up a cell phone store nearby, and I already feel like I need to pull over and rest. The only good thing about this road trip is that it's giving me time to think.

I've asked myself at least a hundred times if this is all worth it. Leaving my life behind instead of just confessing to my sins. Even if I did come clean about everything that happened, I think I'd still leave.

My mom's sister lives in Vegas and we've visited her countless times when I was younger and each time I was there, I told myself that I wanted to live in the city one day. There's something enticing about moving to a place where no one knows you or your past. Where you can blend in with the crowd and not stand out. Dad used to tell me I was born to stand out, and those words alone gave me anxiety.

Minette mountains coat the landscape in the distance. Sunflowers line a field to my right with a beautiful, aged farmhouse that sits beside it. There's a couple of kids running in a sprinkler and I smile at the sight. Seconds pass, and they're gone.

Now my view is a dried-up field with an abandoned house smack dab in the middle of it. The roof is caving in and the windows are all shattered. One might see that old house and consider this area rundown.

Unfortunately, many people see the bad and never take the time to see the beauty in it. Whether it's a town, a home, or a person. Like me. Like Zed. Everyone is so quick to see the ugly that they don't take the time to see anything else. Perception is everything, even if we all have a different reality.

I miss Zed more than I ever have before. For an entire year, I was consumed by him. I was only fifteen years old, but at that age, one person can make up your entire world. After the day he told me, in his exact words, *our paths were meant to cross, but we were never meant to stay on this road,* I knew that I was in too deep. Much deeper than he was. It hurt, but I pulled myself together and moved on from it. Then Luca came along and my attention shifted elsewhere. He was supposed to be my distraction—a new crush.

Even after Luca was gone, I still went back to Zed for a final goodbye.

"He's gone, Zed. Luca is gone." I bury my face into his chest, seeking any ounce of comfort he can offer me. He's the only one who's ever given me any. His way is the only way I know.

He pulls back and looks into my eyes. "Good. Let that rat bastard go back to wherever he came from. You don't need him."

"No," I shake my head. "He didn't go back, Zed. He's dead. Didn't you hear the sirens? He drove straight off the East Street Bridge." Tears fall recklessly down my face. There's no point in sweeping them away, new ones will just keep coming.

"Oh, shit." His eyes widen and he takes a step back. "Suicide?"

"That's what they're saying, but I don't think so. Zed," I look out his window, fearful that someone is watching, "I think Josh did something. I'm scared. Really scared. My parents forked out a buttload of money to keep this all hush-hush and I think they're protecting him."

He waves his hand in the air, blowing out an airy breath. "Nah. Josh is crazy, but to kill someone?"

I look out the window again, continuing to feel like I'm being watched. My fingers wrap around Zed's arm and I pull him away from his bedroom window that faces my house. "Yesterday, Luca told me something. He said that Josh was his former foster brother and while he was staying there, his twin sister fell down the stairs and was in a coma. She woke up not long ago and said that it was Josh who pushed her. Luca came here for Josh, and Josh knew it."

When his eyes roll and he gives me a look like I'm the crazy one, I nudge his shoulder. "Come on, Zed. This can't all be a coincidence. You've seen how Josh is. What if I'm next?"

Two hands plant on my shoulders and Zed's stony eyes look deep into mine. "Listen to me, Vi. I will never let him hurt you. I'll never let anyone hurt you."

His words offer me the warmth I was searching for. "They're sending me to public school. I'm starting on Monday."

"What does school have anything to do with that?"

"Dad thinks that I need to start socializing. I think he's just trying to keep me away from the house. Not that it'll do any good. Josh goes to Redwood High. I'll just see him more."

"Might be good for you, ya know? You've been sheltered your whole life. Get out. Live a little. Make some friends."

I shake my head, no. "I don't need any friends. You're the only friend I need."

Zed runs his fingers through his hair and turns around, giving me his back. "About that. Nothing's changed, Vi. Still don't think it's a good idea for us to be seen together in public."

A lump lodges in my throat. I swallow hard, trying to push it down, but instead, it just brings on more tears. "Why are you so embarrassed by me?"

He spins around so quickly that I feel dizzy just looking at him. "Embarrassed? Is that what you think?"

"Well, why else?"

Warm hands cup my cheeks. He pulls my face so close that our noses brush. "I could never be embarrassed by you, Vi. You're far too perfect. You're far too good for someone like me. The thing is, we're both loaded with enough ammo to destroy one another. I don't wanna hurt you. Not now. Not ever."

"This hurts, Zed," I shout, shoving my hands to his chest a few times. "You're hurting me right now."

He grabs me by the wrist, stopping me, then pulls my chest to his. "Not as bad as I can. I'm not a good guy." He looks into my tear-soaked eyes, but still doesn't care. Has he ever cared? "It has to be this way." His lips press gently to mine in a soft and subtle kiss. He pulls back, and he lets me go.

That was the last time I spoke to Zed up until the night Josh died. There were glances in the halls. *Oh, were there glances.* Those were torturous. It was like every time he passed by me, he poked at my heart a little harder. It got so painful that I learned his routine just so I could avoid him. After some time, he started seeing girls, going to parties, having sex—those were the worst rumors to listen to, but I heard them all. I was an outcast. Hung with the quiet kids in the class beneath him. Overnight, we became exactly what he wanted—complete strangers.

∞

CITY LIGHTS PAINT the picture in front of me. It's just as I remember it. Neon signs, people everywhere—the perfect place to blend in and finally feel free to be myself.

My GPS directs me through the city to the outskirts where Aunt Lisa lives. It's been over a year since I've even seen my aunt, but I don't doubt that we'll be just as close now as we were then. She's the youngest of my mom's siblings, at only thirty-one, and she's a riot. Carefree with a sense of humor and a contagious laugh. If I'm feeling down, Aunt Lisa can always lift me up.

Since I didn't have any of my old cell phone info transferred, out of fear that I'll be tracked down, I don't have any of my contacts. Fortunately, I remember Mom's number, so I call her now to let her know I made it. Even though I'm still ten minutes out.

It goes straight to voicemail, so I leave a message. "Hey, Mom. Just wanted to let you know I'm almost at Aunt Lisa's house. Umm, this is my new number. Save it if ya want. Bye."

Anxiousness swarms my stomach. I smile a real smile for the first time in a while, excited about the possibilities here. Catch up on schoolwork, maybe get a part-time job, graduate, and then the world is my oyster. I've got a trust fund, much like the other brats of Redwood, but I don't even want it. If I could be like anyone, it would be Aunt Lisa. Money changes people, and if I change at all, I only want it to be for the better. After the shit I've done, I certainly can't get much worse.

I pull into the cracked-paved driveway to the small ranch style house that's the same color as a ripe banana with an overhead carport. Similar houses line the road illuminated by the street lights. Once I'm out of the car, I stretch my arms up and listen to the sound of the bass bumping a few houses down.

"Vi!" Aunt Lisa beams as she runs toward me with open arms. She looks exactly the same. In her thirties with the body of a teenager, but much bigger boobs. Chestnut eyes and burnt orange hair that is longer, now almost touching her waist. "It's so good to see you, honey."

I hug her back, falling into the embrace. "You, too. I appreciate you letting me stay here."

She pulls back and takes a look at me. "Of course, I..." Her words trail off as her eyes stare past me.

"What?" I spin around to get a peek at what has her wearing that perplexed look on her face.

My jaw drops, heart in my throat, legs feeling like unbalanced weeds.

"Friend of yours?" Aunt Lisa asks, still watching Zed as he

comes toward us with an expression that's hard to read. "If not, I call dibs." Her brows twitch, and while I wanna smile, I can't.

I can't take my eyes off him as I try to come to terms with the fact that he's here. "Umm, yeah. Can you give us a minute?"

"Of course. I'll get your bag inside and if you need anything, just holler."

I acknowledge her with a nod and wait until she's gone before I meet Zed halfway down the drive. He's stopped, hands in his pockets, and his shoulders slouched.

Zed speaks first, thankfully, because I have no idea what to say to him. "Last time I saw you, you were heading out for coffee. Your aunt must make a killer cup to drive all the way to Nevada."

My arms cross over my chest, and I take a stance with a raised hip. "And last time I saw you, you were ending a call after making an agreement at my expense." I look past him with a suspicious grin. "Are they here? Did you bring 'em with you?"

His brows dip into a deep v. "Who are you even talking about?"

"Come on. Don't play dumb. I heard the entire conversation. Pretty sure your exact words were, *do what I asked and I'll give you what you want.*"

"Ahh, a little eavesdropper. Well, that's exactly why you should never listen in on a phone call. You only get one side of the story."

"So, you're saying that it wasn't about me?" I say with a feeble tone.

"That's exactly what I'm saying. Probably would have helped to ask me before you took off and drove to another state."

Is he lying to me? I can't tell. Suddenly, I feel three inches tall with the defense mechanism of a lioness. It's not my fault; I was born defensive. My mind has been in a constant state of paranoia for the past seven years. "Doesn't matter." I tip my chin up. "We couldn't stay in that hotel forever. This was always my plan, so here I am. You can go now. I think our business is finished." My words are deceitful to my thoughts. I wanna scream at him not to go and to tell me why he cared enough to drive all this way, but I know Zed, and he won't give me anything except short sentences and excuses.

He was right when he said this thing between us was a dead-end. How could I ever stay on the same road as someone who won't show an ounce of his emotions?

We both stand there, an awkward and far too long beat of silence enveloping us. The air is still and calm. Even the bass down the road has stopped.

I swallow hard and wonder if I should just turn around and walk in the house. Maybe he'll stop me, maybe he won't. I can't imagine he came all this way just to make a statement about me going to get coffee.

"Okay, then," I say, dropping my arms, ready to throw in the cards. I shoot a thumb over my shoulder at the house. "I'm just gonna go in. It's been a long day."

As soon as I go to take a step, he stretches his arm between us. "Vi, wait. I need to tell you something." He's not touching me because he's still three feet away, but my movements halt.

"Okay. Say it."

He goes to speak, but closes his mouth. There's an audible breath as his fingertips dig into his eyeballs while he rubs aggressively. Another moment of hesitation, then he finally drops his hands. They hang at his sides and his head shakes. "I don't know how." His voice is timid, almost child-like.

My heart aches for him. As much as I need to hear what he has to say, I'm really not sure if I ever will because I don't think he's capable of forming the sentences. Not because he's dumb, but because he's tortured.

I can't force him to talk. I've tried too many times, and it ends with another piece of my heart getting torn from my chest. I offer him a pinched smile. "Well, when you're ready. You know where to find me."

"Don't go. I can do this." He takes a step closer, looking me dead in the eye. "I'm sorry."

That's it?

"You're sorry? That's what was so hard to say?" My head shakes in disappointment. Here I thought maybe he was on the verge of pouring his heart out to me.

Seemingly taken aback, he rubs his neck, his eyebrows steeped in a frown. "Isn't that enough?"

With a tilted head, I narrow my eyes on him. "Tell me, Zed, what are you sorry for?"

"Fuck, Vi!" he shouts, grabbing his head and spinning on his heels to avoid looking at me. "I haven't apologized to anyone since I was a kid and it was the worst feeling ever. You know I don't like this shit. Feelings, emotions, serious talk." Another long pause, and I'm learning that Zed is the reason I'm such a patient person.

"Everything okay out here?" Aunt Lisa hollers, startling me. Zed still stands there with his back to me and his fingers clenched in his hair.

"Everything's fine. Be in soon," I holler back.

"Okay," Zed huffs, pivoting around and eating up all the space between us. "To start, I'm sorry I kept us a secret. You deserve to be worn like a string of pearls on display for everyone to see. You're beautiful and smart and everything I'm not." He tucks my hair behind my ears and I shiver at his touch.

I bite back a smile, feeling the corners of my eyes prick. That's a really good fucking start, but I don't want praise. "Thanks, I guess." I can feel myself blush and I hate that I'm letting him get to me *again*.

"I don't know, Vi. I could stand here and tell you all the things I'm sorry for, but I'm not sure I can without explaining why I did the things I did. I mean, I'm not the only person who fucked up."

There's no doubt he's talking about me. And he's right. "Okay, then let's get it all out. The good, the bad, and the ugly. Tell me what I did wrong."

"For starters, you gave up too easily," he says point-blankly with a smug look while his shoulders rise and fall.

I blow out a shallow breath. "Are you kidding me right now?"

"No. I'm not kidding. We had it all, and the second I put questions in your head, you walked the other way and never looked back. You didn't so much as look at me for the past two years. And when you did, it was because you needed my help."

Don't slap him. Don't slap him. Don't slap him.

I sweep my hair over my shoulder and hold it to one side, then clear my throat, trying to give myself a second before I say something I'll regret. "Do I need to remind you of those two words you said to me? Hmm... 'Dead-end' ring a bell?" When he doesn't respond, I keep talking. "If anyone gave up, it was you. But how can we blame one another when we didn't even have anything to begin with. We weren't in a relationship. Made no commitments. So yeah, when you made it very clear that you weren't interested, I stepped back. As time went on and you kept living your life perfectly content without me in it, I eventually turned and walked the other way." My voice rises with each word as I grow more and more angry. "I'm not a doormat, Zed. And I certainly won't beg someone for their attention. If you want me in your life, then you fucking tell me and be proud to have me. If not, get the fuck out of here." I sweep my hand in the air and turn around, unable to look at him any longer without really losing my shit.

"I told you the reasons why it wouldn't work back then."

Reclaiming my space right in front of him, I yell, hands flying in the air, "Then how the hell did I give up? Do you hear yourself?"

Using the same high-pitched shout, he finally gives me more. "The next day, you ran to Luca. You fucking kissed him, Vi. And I saw it. Do you have any idea how that made me feel?"

"No. I don't." I poke a finger into his chest with each word that I say. "Because. You. Never. Told. Me." I stop poking him and look him in the eye, feeling like even though we're yelling, we're making progress. "We never stood a chance because you wouldn't ever tell me anything. You gave me nothing to hold on to. And unless you give me something right now, I'm going inside that house and not looking back for the last time."

Immersed in silence, we just stand there. Me, waiting for him to tell me everything I've waited to hear for so long. And him, trying to find the reason not to.

"Come back to Redwood with me. Let me protect you."

"I can't, Zed. I'm sorry." I press my lips together and close my eyes, but the next thing I know, his lips are on mine. His fingers tangle around the back of my head in my mess of hair. My lip ring clanks against his teeth before I open my mouth and invite him in, hoping like hell I don't live to regret it.

CHAPTER SEVENTEEN

ZED

I 've got no idea what I'm doing. But seeing her standing here all vulnerable and inviting, I couldn't resist.

She tastes as sweet as she looks with a fire in her eyes that drives me wild. Vi is all that I want. We could be the only two people left on the planet and I'd be content.

In a dirty driveway in what looks to be a shitty part on the outskirts of Vegas, I eat up this moment. Gripping her hair tightly and devouring her mouth as if it's the last time I'll ever kiss her. That realization pricks at my chest and it's unsettling.

She can't deny this. The way our tongues dance like our favorite song is playing. How our lips fit perfectly together like they were molded just for this kiss. Or, the way both of our hands tremble, hearts race, and palms sweat. It's undeniable. She has to know this.

I retreat and look into her eyes, searching for clarity. "Say something. Anything." Her eyes well with tears. Vi might be the toughest girl I know and she rarely cries, so when she does, I fucking hate it. "Don't cry," I tell her.

"I just don't know what to do anymore. Everything is such a

mess. I really think I should just stay here. I still need to protect myself and if I go back, they'll fry me."

"So, you came here to escape *them*?"

"That's part of it. There's just nothing left for me back in Redwood. I have my aunt here and opportunities that I don't have back home."

She's got a point. Her family sucks about as much as mine does. Not to mention, Redwood is a dumpster for rich kids who just want to live off their parents and trust funds. If you don't move away right out of high school, you pretty much become your parents. "Then I guess I have to move to Vegas." I shrug my shoulders. It's really the only option.

Apparently she finds it funny. Through sniffles, she laughs. "Yeah, right."

"I'm serious."

"Stop it." Her hand hits my shoulder. "You're not staying in Vegas. Don't you have some revenge pact to close back home, anyways?"

"I do. And I will." I grab her by the waist and pull her to me. Looking down at her, I negotiate. "How about this? I'm gonna go get a room for the night and I'll come back in the morning. We can talk then."

"I just need more time to think about everything."

"Time? Okay. I can do that." I don't want to, but I'll give her some time. "Like I said, I'll get a hotel in the city and come back in the morning."

"Zed," she huffs out my name, "I don't mean a night, or even a couple days. I just need time to think about all of this. It's not just you, or us, it's everyone else, too."

"Fuck everyone else."

She looks down at her feet and cracks a smile. "That's such a Zed thing to say."

"At one time, it was a Vi thing to say, too."

"Maybe I've changed."

I side-eye her in question. "Have you?" Vi is like a chameleon. She adapts to her surroundings and behaves in a way that fits the moment. She can be so sweet in one situation and a raging storm in another. She's fire and ice—oil and water. Heinz 57—a little bit of everything.

"I'm trying. Just like you wanna be better, I do, too."

"Only for you. I don't give a damn about anyone else, and I say that with one hundred percent certainty."

"What about your friends?"

With an unrestrained smirk, I tell her the truth, knowing she's the only person who will ever hear it. "I always have my boys' backs, and I'm pretty sure they'll always have mine, but too much shit has happened and I don't think we can ever go back to the way things were. I'm the castoff, the unfixable, the one they pity and loathe." My hands slide in my front pockets and my shoulders rise. "It is what it is. Life goes on."

Vi bites the inside of her cheek and looks at me while deep in thought.

A few seconds later, she finally speaks. "It's my fault. You were all so close until I came back into your life."

My hand waves through the air and I push those thoughts away. "Nah. Don't think like that. We were bound to break apart eventually. Come on, how many people stay close with their childhood friends their entire lives?"

She doesn't say anything, but I'm sure she's still blaming herself. It doesn't matter, because soon this will all be over. Soon, they'll have what they want and I'll have my peace. We can all finally move on with our lives.

"I really should get inside. My aunt is probably wondering what the hell is going on out here. I'd invite you in, but it's just... sort of weird, considering I'm a guest myself."

"Yeah, don't worry about it. I'll get a hotel, though, and I'll be back tomorrow." I lean forward and kiss her cheek, feeling her cheekbones rise as I hold my lips in place. "Night, Vi."

"Goodnight, Zed."

∞

My phone buzzing on top of my chest wakes me up, from what I consider the best night sleep I've had in months.

I lift my phone, crane my neck and read the message from the home screen.

Lars: Papers have been delivered.

I shoot him a text back.

Me: Good. See ya Saturday night.

I'm over all this shit, but that doesn't mean I'm giving up. We've come this far, might as well see everything to the end.

It won't be long now. Soon, I can go to my dad with the contract I had drawn up by my attorney and everything will be transferred over to me, everything but his house and his shitty business, that's slowly going down the drain. This contract gives me ownership of everything my mom owned before she passed away. The house isn't one of those things. If I wanted to get really greedy, I could force it out of him, but my attorney advised against it.

Not that I want it. That house is full of so many awful memories—affairs on my dad's part, deceit, and a murder. That's exactly what it was. My mom was slowly being murdered by my dad and she didn't even know it was happening.

He had that house built and never even let her have a say in how anything was done. He was always so cruel to her and I never even noticed until it was too late. She never even got the funeral she deserved. He made up some shit about how she always said she didn't want people to cry over her death when she passed and that she'd prefer to just have a celebration of life— well, he never gave her that either. It's like one minute she was here, and the next, we were burying her with only close friends and the only family Dad and I have, my grandma.

It's not possible to bring her back, but I can avenge her death and serve justice by shredding him of his dignity, and his soul.

After I call the concierge and have a travel toothbrush and toothpaste delivered to my room, I go into the bathroom to get cleaned up. It's a pretty nice hotel for a last-minute reservation. If I'd known I'd be staying the night, I would have brought extra clothes, but everything happened on a whim, so I'll be wearing the same clothes I had on yesterday until I get back to my hotel in Redwood.

So many hotels, random houses, and different towns lately. I'd like to say the travels have been rejuvenating, but that's not the case at all.

Not even bothering to check out, I just leave my key card on the bed and head back over to Vi's aunt's house.

Of all the talking we did last night, she never once asked me how I found her. Guess she's just getting used to the fact that she can run but she can't hide. I'd go to the ends of the earth to get to her.

I'm actually really surprised I was even able to get it out of her mom. Talking to Mrs. Moran was sort of preparation for everything I said to Vi. I had to lay it all out there. Told her I cared about her daughter and wanted her to be happy. In return, she told me she suspected it all along. She actually told me that she felt as if I brought Vi to life. At the end of the conversation, she threatened me and told me how much she loves her daughter. I just wish she'd tell that to Vi—I'm not so sure she knows.

For the first time in a long time, it feels as though everything is falling into place. The weight off my shoulders is insane. It's been two tortuous years of fighting against my feelings. I convinced myself of so many fallacies. The biggest of all was that Vi would be a constant reminder of the pain I endured in the past, just because she was there. Instead of pushing her away, we could have shared in the pain and healed together.

Blinking rapidly, I look up and down the street as I stop in front of Vi's aunt's. This has to be it. It's the same house I was at last night, but the only car in the driveway is the one under a carport.

Maybe Vi ran out for coffee or breakfast.

Regardless, I get out of my truck and walk up the short driveway. Once I'm at the door, I knock a few times then turn around to take in the scenery of the neighborhood while I wait. Last night, I was convinced that this area was rundown, but in the daylight, it's not so bad. Although the houses are bunched together and the color of them is godawful.

The door cracks open, so I spin back around. "Hey, I'm a friend of Vi's. Is she around?"

Lisa tugs her robe around her and wipes at her eyes, and I'm given the impression that I woke her up. "No, she actually left early this morning. Said she'd call me and let me know when she's coming back."

"She what?" I throw my head back and exhale all the air from my lungs in one heavy breath. "Damnit," I mutter under my breath.

"It's nice to meet you, but maybe you can come back another time when she's here and we can do the whole formal introduction. I'm working the night shift tonight and really need my z's."

"Yeah, sure." I turn around and walk away without another word.

Damnit! Where the hell is she going now?

This girl is a fucking tornado and I'm getting whiplash from her constant running.

CHAPTER EIGHTEEN

Once I'm out of the city, I pull over to the side of the road to make a call. Fortunately, I was able to track down Adaline's number after a short web search.

It's been six months since I've spoken to her, and we made a deal that we'd never speak again. But I have to reach out this one last time.

I'm not surprised when it rings a couple times, then goes to voicemail. I don't answer unknown calls either. My best bet is to leave a message, so she knows it's me, and hopefully, she'll call back.

After the beep, I give it my best shot. "Hi, Adaline. It's Vi. I know calling you goes against everything we promised, but I really need to talk to you. Don't worry, everything is fine. Just please call me back at this number. It's a new phone, untraceable, and unfortunately, I don't know the number, so hopefully it popped up on your caller ID. Umm, okay. Thanks. Bye."

I end the call and wait.

Minutes pass and she doesn't call back. I tap my fingers on the steering wheel to the beat of "Black" by Pearl Jam, and wait just a little longer.

Cars pass by and each one gives my car a shake, making me think I should have pulled over a little further. A trucker lays on the horn, startling me, and for some reason, memories of that night stampede into my head like a bad nightmare.

It has to be here, somewhere. I pull out every drawer and sift through them in search of the bag I watched Josh get from a local drug dealer. I'm not sure what it was, but I definitely plan to find out.

My heart is pounding forcefully in my chest, rattling my rib cage, and causing my entire body to break out in a cold sweat.

"Come on, where is it?" I mutter under my breath as I toss things around.

It's not in here. I slam the drawers shut and drop to my knees to look under the bed.

Spotless. Not even a stray sock.

Just as I go to stand up, something catches my eye. It's a metal clasp on a box tucked under the bed. There's some strange engraving on it, an infinity symbol, maybe? As I lie on my side, with half of my body under the bed, I stretch my arm underneath the bed and move my hand around until I get a good grip on it. Once I've got it, I pull it down and slide out.

In one swift motion, I pop the clasp and open it up.

Bingo.

Sitting in the box is a bottle of pills with the word 'Desoxyn 5mg' written with black marker.

Underneath the pill container are some folded-up papers. I slap the box shut and get to my feet.

I've gotta get out of here before he catches me.

Looking both ways down the hall, I make a beeline for my room. As soon as I'm inside, I close the door, lock it, and slide down until my ass is on the floor.

Flipping the clasp, I open the box. I set the pills beside me and pull out the folded-up papers.

Then I see it.

My heart drops while nausea coils around it in my stomach.

That's Marni Thorn—in her bedroom. I pull out the picture, then another and another. There are at least a dozen pictures of her taken unknowingly.

He's sick. Really fucking sick.

I set them aside and unfold the first paper. My eyes skim over Josh's handwriting.

"Oh, no!" I grumble. These aren't notes—this is a plan. A plan of attack. Dates and all.

Starting with tomorrow night.

I pile everything back into the box, lock it shut, and search my room high and low for a place to hide it where Josh won't find it.

I come up empty-handed. If Josh wants something, he will find it. He's torn my room up from top to bottom in search of random things— my journal, my phone, my car keys. Anything he wants that feeds his sick compulsive tendencies at the time.

With the box in hand, I go over to my closet and grab a drawstring bag, then drop it in. I throw a couple shirts on it for safe measure, then leave my room and the house before he gets home.

Once I'm in the car, I pull my phone out and text Adaline.

Me: I need your help. Josh is up to something. I think he's planning on hurting someone. I think you should come here. Text me back ASAP.

Me: P.S. Delete this message after you read it.

I'm driving from one back road to the next in search of somewhere to hide this box where no one will ever find it.

Somehow, I end up at Briarwood. An old asylum outside of town. The sight of the dilapidated building alone gives me the creeps.

I'm pretty sure there are random parties here on the weekends, especially with Halloween right around the corner, but I'm sure I can find a spot where no one will ever look. Even if I have to dig a hole myself.

My phone rings, snapping me out of the dreadful memory of that day.

"Adaline," I say as soon as I take her call. "Thank God, listen. We need to talk."

"I thought we had a deal. Never speak again." Her voice is tranquil, yet stern.

"We did. But there's something you need to know. I'm confessing."

"Like hell you are!" she screams, now using a high-pitched roar that has me drawing in a deep breath and holding it while I listen. "We had a deal. If you do this, I'll deny everything. Don't think for a second I'm taking the fall—"

"Adaline, stop!" I cut her off. "I'm not going to the cops. I'm going to those guys I told you about. The ones who are friends with Zed—the guy who helped us. They've managed to throw themselves into this mess and have been trying to put all the puzzle pieces together. They know I was on that app and talking to Josh the night he died. I have to tell them the truth about what happened."

"No! Just let it go, Vi."

"You don't understand. I have to do this. You get to live your perfect life over there in California. I don't. I'm front and center and I'm fucking miserable." A lump rises in my throat and the corners of my eyes sting, threatening tears.

"Living a perfect life? You think that's what I'm doing. I'm in a wheelchair. Paralyzed for the rest of my life. I'll never walk again because of Josh. I'm alive, but I'd hardly call it living the perfect life. Not to mention, my brother is dead because of him. Remind your conscience of that next time it comes knocking."

Releasing a breath, I rest my head back and take a minute to think. But no matter what outcomes play out in my mind, it all comes back to just getting this over with and telling the guys everything I know. They'll do with the information what they will, but at least I'll be free of the chains I've tied to myself. "I didn't call to negotiate. I called to tell you what I'm doing and to let you know that I'll never mention your name or Zed's. Same goes for Luca's. I don't know you. You don't know me." With that, I end the call and fill my lungs with a shallow breath.

It went pretty much as I expected. She just needed to know that I won't incriminate her. Adaline has been through a lot and the last thing she needs is to worry about any of this. She's right, though, Josh did end up getting what he deserved.

I pack the dirt down over the top of the box, just to the left of the asylum. Six steps horizontal, six steps vertical. It should be safe here until I figure out what to do with this information. I left everything but the pills inside of it. I need to research what they are and then flush them down the toilet before Josh ever has a chance to slip them to someone—someone I take to be Marni.

As soon as I turn around, my eyes bug out, jaw dropping, heart pounding.

"Zed? Umm, what are you doing here?" He stands at the corner of the building with his hands in the front pocket of his jeans and his ankles crossed. A cigarette dangles from the corner of his tipped-up smirk.

"Could ask you the same thing. Whatcha hiding over there?"

I'm pretty sure all the blood has drained from my face. There's no doubt in my mind I've been caught. "Goldfish died. Figured I should give him the proper send-off to wherever goldfish go."

"Ya know you can just flush those things down the toilet and they'll go to the same place?"

I take a few steps toward him with my eyes on my car. "I'd never. That's so inhumane." I need to get him out of here before he digs up the box. My phone vibrates in my back pocket, so I pull it out. It's a text from Adaline.

I continue to walk as I read the messages, with Zed following behind me.

Adaline: I'm coming to Redwood. Be there in a couple hours. It's time we stop this asshole once and for all.

I thumb a text back to her quickly.

Me: I agree. Hurry.

Sweeping my eyes left and right, I try to get a look at him in my peripheral, but don't see him. I can sense he's near, so I'm pretty sure he's directly behind me.

When his warm breath hits the nape of my neck, I jump. "Where ya going?" he says, as if it's just a casual question from one friend to another.

"Home," I quip.

"Right. Probably gotta clean up that fish tank. Ya know, since your fish died and all."

"Exactly." I reach my car and open the door before turning to face him. "Have a good one, Zed." That ache from years ago suddenly hits me like a tidal wave. Full force and smack dab in the center of my chest, taking my breath away. I've looked into those eyes countless times and it never gets easier.

"I'll come along. I know those things can get heavy with all that water." He heads for the passenger door, but I jog up to him and grab his arm.

"No. My dad's there. He can help later."

With his gaze locked on my hand that's wrapped around his wrist, he tsks, "Come on, Vi. We both know there's no fish. Not to mention, you're a terrible liar. If you're ever a suspect of a crime, your best bet is to just run away."

Dropping my hand, I cross my arms over my chest and grimace. "Okay, you caught me. There's no fish. I was just taking a walk to think and pushing down mole holes. Now, could we just get out of here?"

"You're free to go wherever you want. This is my sanctuary. My reprieve, if you will." He brushes his fingers in the air giving me a scoot. "Go on. Run away like you always do."

Swallowing hard, I take a few steps back with my eyes still locked on his. He's not lying. I do run away from him, but not for the reasons he thinks. I don't avoid him because I hate him; I do it because I don't.

I've got no choice, so I get back in my car. There's a good chance he didn't even see me bury the box. Pretty sure he just walked up as I was patting it down with my foot.

I shift into drive, watching him until he's no longer in sight.

It seems nothing's changed. He still gets under my skin in the best and worst way.

That night, Adaline arrived in town and got a room at the inn, so I stayed with her to avoid the house. Josh must have noticed his box was missing because Mom called saying that he was looking for me and then proceeded to break every glass object in the house.

The next day we went to dig up the box and it was gone. Zed found it. He took it and he never even called me to ask what the hell it was. He thought it was me. He thought I made those plans.

I created a fake account on this app that Josh was using to stalk Marni, or watch her, rather. I pretended to be another guy who was obsessed with Marni. Sparked a conversation and he talked about how he has this urge to touch her. How he likes when women fight back. It made my skin crawl, but I had to play along with it. Then he said he was doing it that night. He was ready to put his plan in action and kidnap Marni.

Now, Adaline needs to trust me. I'm making the right choice.

CHAPTER NINETEEN

ZED

I'm back in Redwood and walking through the house I once called home. I don't even knock as I push open the door to my dad's study.

"Surprised it took you so long to call," I say to the man in front of me. His feet are kicked up on top of the messy desk. Scattered papers lie on the floor, a couple dirty glasses stained with the bronze bourbon he drinks sit in front of him on the desk. He grabs one that's half full and tips it back.

Glaring at me, he hits the buzzer on his phone. "Bring me another." He proceeds to press the buzzer again. "Actually, make that two. My son is here."

"Yes, sir," Marie, the housekeeper, says through the speaker.

Once he pushes the empty glasses out of the way, his attention shifts back to me. "So, what's this shit you're trying to pull?"

I set the folder I brought along in front of me on his desk. He eyeballs it, but doesn't say anything. "Not really sure what you're talking about? I'll need you to explain further."

His feet drop and he bends down to grab something. When he comes back up, he slaps a folder to the table. "Is that explanation enough for you?"

"I've got no idea what that is," I lie. It's the folder I've kept for two years. The same one I had the guys deliver to King Corp.

"Listen, boy. We can talk in circles all day. Just tell me what the fuck you think this proves?"

With a clenched jaw, I flip the folder open and shuffle through the papers that I've looked at, at least a dozen times. "Looks to me like you murdered my mother," I say calmly, keeping my temper in check.

In a rapid movement, he slams the folder shut. "You've got nothing here. Some pics of me taking care of my sick wife. Trying to help her in the best way I knew how. Quit trying to make something out of nothing."

I laugh. Deep, dark, and malicious. Each eruption of breath from my vocal chords laced with intent that only drives me deeper into the rage that has consumed me. Striking my fist to the desk, I look him dead in the eye, my patience taking a back seat to my fury. "Listen, you piece of flushed shit, I know what you did. You know what you did. And it's time for you to tell me why."

He laughs in reply, trying to intimidate me, but I can sense the fear in him. I can see it, and if I were able to, I could touch it. It's apparent and he can't hide it, no matter how hard he tries. "I've got nothing left to say to you. It's apparent you've chosen your side and you'll believe what you need to believe to work through your grief. I've already contacted my attorney and he's advised me to cut a deal, just to save face for our family's sake. We've been through enough already." He pulls open a drawer and retrieves his checkbook. With a drop of it onto the table, he pops the top of his pen. "How much do you need?"

I smirk, raise my shoulders, and respond, "All of it."

The pen hits the table and his head falls back as more laughter spews out. "You're funny. Now seriously, how much?"

"All of it." Leaning forward with my palms pressed to the

desk, I get in his face. "Do what your attorney advised and give me everything that was hers. That's my deal."

This old man has no fucking idea that his attorney is working for me. I've promised him a hefty amount to steer dear old dad in the right direction. I knew the first thing he would do is seek legal advice. I also know he can't make a decision for himself, even if it's something as simple as choosing between ranch and Italian dressing.

A knock at the door has Dad looking past me. "Come in, Marie."

She enters with a serving tray and two filled glasses. Without a word, she sets them down on the desk and takes the dirty ones away.

Dad grabs his, swirling the contents as the ice clanks against the glass. "I'll give you fifty mil," he says, before taking a long swig of his bourbon.

"All of it," I deadpan.

"Sixty."

"You can keep your house and anything in it that's not mine or hers. I'll even be generous enough to let you keep King Corp. I want all of her accounts that you took ownership of signed over to me. Every single penny that you did not earn is mine."

"Seventy."

This fucker just doesn't stop. Fortunately, I expected it. Unfortunately for him, I don't back down, so I decline his offer once more. "All of it, or I call my attorney and tell him to proceed with a lawsuit. Then, I'll take this to the investigator who opened and closed the case of her death in a matter of minutes."

Tipping his glass back, he takes every last drop. Even as it's emptied, he still holds the brim of the glass to his lips. Seconds later, he finally sets it back down. "My own flesh and blood. Such a shame."

"I could say the same about you. I've always known you were a greedy bastard, but to take everything from my mom and not even name your only son as the beneficiary." Heat festers inside of me, bringing my blood to a boiling point. "Yeah," I nod, "I know. You planned on giving everything to a godson you hardly even know. A twenty-seven-year-old chump who already has enough money to buy anything his heart desires. He's a fucking major league baseball player." Slapping my hands down on the table in front of me, jaw ticking, and heart fucking pounding. "I'm your fucking son!"

He doesn't even blink before jumping to his feet. Putting his hands right in front of mine, he leans forward and shouts, "That's right. Because that kid deserves it. He's smart and chases his dreams. He's going places." He blows out a breath of laughter. "Unlike you. You'll throw this money away on stupid shit because you lack the brain cells to make logical choices. You're worthless, a waste of space."

I shake a finger at him and withdraw eye contact. "You went too fucking far." My lip curls up in disgust as I crank my clenched fist back and unload right on his nose. Knuckle meeting bone, as blood trickles on top of the folder I brought with me. Grabbing a damp napkin on his desk from one of his many shots of bourbon, I wipe the blood off the folder, then toss it at him. His hands cup his nose and he doesn't say a word as he looks at me in complete shock that I had the nerve to hit him.

I flip open the blood-streaked folder and pull out the agreement I had my attorney draw up. "Sign this. Then you have twenty-four hours to get everything switched over. If you don't, I'll proceed with legal action." I drop the paper in front of him that already has my signature.

"I'm not signing that shit. At least not until my attorney looks over it," he says in a muffled tone, as he continues to catch the dropping blood from his nose.

I smirk, knowing that would be his response. "Alright then, you better get to it. Twenty-four hours." My fingers wrap around the cold glass of bourbon Marie brought me. I tip it back, taking it down in one gulp, and slam the glass to the desk. "Twenty-four hours." I snap my fingers at him. Slow strides lead me to the door, the smile on my face growing more and more with each step.

He can seek all the advice he needs from his attorney. Mr. Mitchum has already been told to push my dad to sign the agreement. And there's no doubt in my mind he'll do it. It might not be the punishment he deserves, but this is only the start.

Hook. Line. Sinker.

CHAPTER TWENTY

I'm not exactly sure what's going on when I pull into the driveway at my house. Mom is wearing a long pair of rubber gloves and hovering over a plant that sits in a large black bucket. The leaves are wilted and crisp, and the expression on her face matches the sorrow in the sorry-looking plant.

"Umm, Mom. Is everything okay?" I ask her as I close the door of my car and greet her on the lawn. Has she officially gone off the deep end? Is this the part of my story where I realize my mom needs to be committed?

With her hands pressed to her hips and the fingers of the gloves hanging loosely, she eyeballs the plant. "This darn plant. It's been in the back yard since Josh's service and I figured it was time to try and bring it back to life."

"Because..." I drag out the word, "you think that it will bring Josh back to life?" My brows shoot to my forehead and I realize that this very well could be that part of my story.

"No, silly." She swats my arm with a strange curve to her lips —a smile, maybe? "I just feel so bad that it's been back there dying and thought maybe I'd try to plant it."

I look around the yard in search of the gardener. I mean, he has to be here to help her. Mom certainly doesn't have a green thumb. In fact, I don't think she's ever planted anything in her life. "Where's Leo? Is he helping you with this?"

"Nope. This is my own little project." She grabs a shovel and sticks the tip of it right into some fresh grass about three feet from the flower garden in front of the house.

"Whoa, whoa, whoa." I grab the shovel. "Let's not do this in the middle of the yard. Wouldn't it look better mixed in the flower beds?"

Tapping her finger to her chin, she looks over at the flower beds. "Hmm. I suppose you're right." She lets the shovel drop to the ground and a look of defeat replaces the hopefulness she was wearing.

"Come on. I'll help you." I bend down and grab the shovel. There's an open spot between some fresh flowers. There's a bunch of mulch around them and probably one of those barriers underneath that. Fortunately, it looks like she did grab some gardening scissors. "Hand me those scissors." I push away the mulch and clear a spot, then start cutting at the black weed barrier.

"Where did you learn how to do this?" she asks me, surprised with my ability to cut netting.

"I used to watch a lot of home and garden shows when I was homeschooled." That was a time in my life when I was always home. My parents kept me so sheltered then, and now, I feel like they just want me to fly away.

As I'm cutting and pulling, moving mulch, and making the hole, I start the conversation I came here for. "Mom," I say, skeptically, "I'd like to talk about him."

Mom grabs a rubber kneeling mat and sets it down beside me. With her gloves still on, she kneels down on it. "About Josh?"

"Mmmhmm." I nod, avoiding eye contact, and continuing my work on this hole. We've never really talked about him. For some reason, she's so defensive of the boy. We've had five different kids come in from foster homes—Luca being the last—but she took to Josh in a way that she never even took to me. Before I go to the guys and tell them the truth, I need to tell my mom why I hated him so much, even if I don't plan on telling her what I did.

My truth may go public, and I'd rather her know my reasoning now versus after she finds out what I did.

"I'm glad you want to talk about him, Vi. I really am. Because I'd like to talk about him, too."

Pressing my lips together, I nod and look at her, an odd feeling washing over me. This is not us. Mom and I do not have meaningful conversations. Perhaps we're both growing and changing for the better. "Okay, you start."

She reaches out and grabs the bucket and slides the plant toward me once I have the hole dug. I start loosening the roots as she talks. "I know you and Josh didn't get along the best. He was a bit...hard to handle. But you can't blame him. He behaved the only way he knew how."

Here we go again. I get to hear about how perfect Josh was. And I thought that maybe, just maybe, this talk would help to ease some of my guilt and shine some truth as to who Josh really was.

"Mom, stop." I hold up a hand. My eyes close and my head drops. "Just stop. I'm not sure what you remember, but Josh wasn't just a bit hard to handle. He was dangerous, reckless, and if he were still alive, we'd probably all be dead. He was not a good person and he never had good intentions."

"Vi Moran! Do not talk about your late brother that way. We will honor his memory."

I can't do this. I push the plant away and brush my bare legs off. "I can't do this." Heart aching, I push myself off the ground. It hurts too bad to know that she is this delusional.

"I thought you wanted to talk about your brother," she says with puzzlement.

"Quit calling him that!" I shout, much louder than I planned.

"He was not my brother. He will never be my brother. I hate him, Mom. I really do."

"He was your brother," she whimpers before her face falls into her gloved hands. "He *is* your brother. And he always will be."

"No! He's not!" I yell over her stifled cries.

"But he is. Josh is my son. My real son. I gave birth to him at a small hospital in California on March seventeenth, two thousand and two. A beautiful blue-eyed, nine-pound baby boy."

"No," I grumble, shaking my head. "That's not true."

She lifts her head and stares past me as if the memory is playing in her head like a movie. "I remember not hearing him cry. I thought something was wrong, but then I heard that beautiful sound and they laid him on my chest."

"You're lying," I spit out, unable to comprehend what she's saying. Josh isn't my brother.

Sad eyes peer back at me. Red-rimmed and coated with tears. "He is. Josh is my son. Right before I met your dad, I fell in love with a sailor—or at least I thought I did. He was striking. With ocean blue eyes and sun-kissed skin. Wavy blond hair and strong hands. I fell under his spell, and he kept me there. Once I found out I was pregnant, he became abusive and cruel. I knew I couldn't bring a child into that world. I had no choice but to run away, only days before I was due to give birth. I told the agency I didn't know who the dad was and I signed off my rights to him. They assured me he would go to a good home."

Not even realizing my hand was clapped over my mouth, I drop it to my side. "You're serious?"

"Very serious." She grabs the plant and pulls it from the bucket, shaking off the excess soil. "I said my goodbyes and kept running until I came to Arizona. I met your dad only two months later and got pregnant with you. He proposed, I said yes, and the rest is history."

"How...how did you find Josh?"

Once the roots are set in the hole, she begins filling the dirt back in. "Years of searching. I never stopped looking. I was in constant contact with different agencies. That's how I became so invested in giving these kids better lives, even if most were just temporary."

"Does Dad know?"

She nods. "He does. And he was accepting of my decision. He knew that I loved Josh very much. That's why he put up with his behavior. Even when he was ready to call quits on our marriage because he became so fed up, he chose me, and choosing me meant keeping Josh."

I grab the black bucket and move it out of the way. "And me? Did he know that I'm his sister?"

"He did. I suspect that's why he was so angry all the time. You got the life he didn't—and I gave it to you, but took it away from him."

I believe her. It all makes sense now. But it doesn't change the way I feel. "Regardless of whether he was your child or not, Josh was dangerous, Mom. You put our entire family at risk."

Sobbing, she completely breaks down. "I just wanted to make it up to him. I wanted to be his mom again. He was tossed in and out of so many homes and endured so much abuse. And that pastor," her head shakes as she whisks the stray strands of hair from her wet cheeks, "he hurt my boy."

He didn't, though. He didn't hurt Josh. He hurt me.

"No, Mom. Pastor Jeffries never touched Josh."

"He did, though, honey. The investigator closed the case for good last week. It was concluded that Rick Jeffries drugged Josh, and when he escaped, that sick pastor chased him down and hit him. That man touched my boy and then killed him before killing himself."

I wanna scream the truth. Tell her that it was all a setup on the pastor. That Josh was not a part of it. But, I can't. Without incriminating myself, I can't say any of it.

Instead, I drop down beside her, put an arm over her shoulder, and I let her grieve the loss of her son. Josh is gone and he can't hurt us anymore, but she never felt threatened. She only saw her flaws and how she failed him. To her, he was a good kid. I'll let her hold on to that. She deserves it.

She'll never know the truth.

CHAPTER TWENTY-ONE

ZED

It's been two days since I picked up the signed agreement from my dad. Two days since the accounts were transferred to me, making me richer than sin.

I still haven't heard from Vi. I went to her house to talk to her mom, but no one was home. Went back again, and the house-keeper told me they went on vacation.

Vacation! We're in the middle of a crisis and Vi takes a fucking vacation with her family. The guys delivered and are fully expecting me to follow through with my end of the deal and I have every intention of doing just that.

When I pull up to Briarwood, I'm not surprised at all to see a party in full swing. It's not even dusk and the place is crawling with people, ranging from juniors in high school to juniors in college. The front door is wide open, shining light into the decayed building. Jogging up the steps, I stop and take in the engraving on the handle. *Our symbol.* To this day, the guys still have no idea that the symbol of our pact, our friendship—one that's tattooed on our skin for eternity—came from the guy who spun this merry-go-round.

The day I found that box, I was convinced that Vi was after

Marni. Figured she just had some jealous vendetta against her or maybe a sick chick crush. Couldn't give two shits less. Once Vi called me and told me what she had done, I acted fast. Got right in my grandma's old car with every intention of scraping that boy off the road and getting rid of his body myself. It had crossed my mind that someone might get to him before I did; I just never would have guessed it would be Talon and Tommy. I got the call from Lars to come pick him up because the guys needed us and that's when I knew: they got there before me.

Talon had this grand idea and I ran with it. Make Anderson Thorn think he hit Josh. Then everything started to fall apart from that point on.

It wasn't until later that night when the dust settled and I was sitting in the basement of this building with a dead body that I started to put two and two together. Vi wasn't after Marni, Josh was. Talon told us all Josh was obsessed with the girl. I went to the side of the building, dug that box up again and kept it, knowing it would come in handy one day. The papers are still there, probably weathered and worn by now.

As I was packing up a surprise to leave for our friend Marni— the first phase of Talon's act of revenge—the guys noticed the engraving. That day, we all got tattoos. Tommy went to town and started branding everything with it. It was a symbol of our pact: from start to finish and everything in between.

We're still in the in-between. It's not finished yet.

When I step inside, I immediately spot Lars and Willa. She sticks out like a sore thumb and I'm still in awe of the fact that this guy is about to be a dad. "What's up, man?" Lars slaps a hand in mine then bumps my fist.

I know these guys still can't stand me, but tonight is all for show. They know the routine, we've done this more times than I can count.

"You good?" Lars asks me, seeking assurance. He's got no idea why I called this reunion. No one does, and they don't need to.

"I'm fucking great. Need to talk to you guys, though. Meet me outside in five." I slap a hand to his shoulder, stepping past him. Willa puts a hand on her stomach and steps aside, letting me pass by.

There's a herd of girls in front of me, snubbing their noses up at their surroundings. "This place is so creepy. Let's go out by the fire," one of them says.

As they go to walk out, I catch up to them and throw my arm in front of the open frame of the back door. "Fire's for VIP only for the next twenty minutes. Stay in the house or go out front."

"Who made you the groundskeeper?" A cocky little brunette snarls, reminding me all too much of the other brunette in my life. I like her moxie, but she needs to save that shit for someone who cares.

I grab her by the waist, hoist her up, and carry her through the house until we reach the front door that I just walked in three minutes ago. Her eyes about bug out of their sockets as her friends chase after me. "Put me down," she screams, kicking her feet and hitting me, but not fazing me in the least.

"Zed!" Willa huffs from the sidelines, but I ignore her, too.

Once I hit the first concrete step, I set her down. "Don't test me, little girl. Go out front, drink yourself stupid, or leave. Signed, the groundskeeper." Taking a step back until I'm inside the house, I flash her a wink to hold on to. *Stupid fucking girls.*

I can hear them whispering and giggling as I walk back the same way I came from, my arms lighter this time.

As soon as I'm in the back yard, I cup my hands over my mouth. "Everyone out front." When they search the property, wondering who the asshole yelling is, I shout louder, "Right fucking now!"

A few catch sight of me and scramble around the side of the house. But a string of dumbasses just stand there gawking and gossiping while they sip on the keg beer that *I* fucking bought. "You assholes hard of hearing?" I snatch one cup, then two, then three, dropping them to the ground and spilling their beer. "I said, out front. There's a private party back here for the next half hour so get lost."

"Yeah. We're good." Jace, a senior and football player at Redwood, smirks before turning back to his friends and pretending like I'm not standing here ready to decapitate him.

With a heavy boot, I step on the red plastic cups, cracking them and grinding them into the ground. "Alright. I see we have to go about this in a more childish manner. I'll give you until the count of three before I pull your underwear over the back of your fucking head and kick your ass into that fire."

"Come on, man. Let's just go," one of the smaller ones says—Mitch, I think is his name. *Smart guy.*

Jace blows out a murky, beer-infused breath of laughter. "Fuck this guy."

Deep breath in, short breath out, I nudge his shoulder with mine. Our noses brush as my eyes take in his. "One."

He laughs.

"Two."

He's tensing up now that his friends have ditched him.

"Three."

With two hands, I spin him around, grab the fringe of his boxers, and pull. He squirms and tries to fight me off, but I tug harder and harder until the fucking things rip, never making it to his head.

Two hands hit my chest, shoving me back. I crouch down and charge at him, slamming his back to the ground. "Seems like you need to invest in polyester. Those cheap cotton ones don't fly around here."

"Get the fuck off me," he bellows from beneath me. Acting like a fucking pussy, he grabs a fistful of my hair and pulls, so I do the only thing I can think of and nail my forehead to his.

"You're a fucking psycho." He rolls out from underneath me and I let him go, hoping he learned his lesson.

"Yeah, I am. Remember that next time I tell you to do something at my party."

He looks at me in astonishment, as if he didn't know this was my party. Of course he does. Most everyone knows that the parties here are thrown by me and the guys; therefore, it's mine, it's Tommy's, it's Lars', and it's Talon's.

"Really, Zed. We can't have one party without you raising hell?" Tommy says, smacking me on the back of the head.

"I fucking hate people." I really do. I'm not sure how I ever survived all those years of school.

Tommy hands me a full cup of beer, then takes a sip of his own. "Well, lucky for you, the feelings are mutual. People hate you, too"

"Good. Maybe they'll leave me the hell alone."

I throw an arm around Tommy's shoulder, knowing that he's one of the three that can still stand me. We walk up to the fire and wait for the others to join us.

"How's things with Wyatt going?" I ask him.

"Really good. Never been happier."

I nod, taking a drink. "I'm glad. You deserve it. You all do."

"So do you, Zed."

I sweep the air with my hand. "Nah, happiness is overrated. I'd much rather be alone and miserable for the rest of my life."

Tommy laughs at my response. "Keep telling yourself that. One day you might believe it."

"I dunno, man. I think I'm just growing tired of all the bullshit. I'm ready for something mellow and drama-free. Maybe an escape to the mountains off the coast, where I'm not tempted to murder anyone just for talking."

"Honestly, I think that's exactly what you need."

We both laugh again, then simultaneously look over to the building when we hear Lars and Talon coming toward us.

Talon raises his cup and hollers, "Reunited once again."

"Oh shit, he's drunk," I say to Tommy, who nods in agreement.

"He started around noon today. He's fucking shit-faced."

"Where's Marni?" I ask, now utterly confused as to why she's not here. She's one of us, after all.

"A bit of advice for you, Zeddy Bear." Talon throws an arm over my shoulder. He reeks of beer and liquor, maybe even something fruity. "Don't put your girl in charge of the keg. You can't leave her side because everyone with a dick eye-fucks her and you just hang out guarding her ass, filling your cup over and over again." We all convulse in laughter until Talon reaches in his pocket and pulls out something. His mouth practically touches my ear as he whispers, "I saved one. Knew it would come in handy one day." He grabs my hand and slaps it in. "Do your fucking thing."

With a tight fist, I stick my hand in my pocket, drop the match in, then pat him on the back. "Thanks."

On a whim, I called Talon last night. There was no hate or blame. No he said/she said. It was a real conversation between two childhood friends. All bullshit aside, I asked him for permission to talk to Marni in private tonight. He gave me his blessing and I gave him a hint at my plan.

Over the last six months, there's been a lot of bad blood among me and the guys, but when it all comes down to it, we'd bleed for one another. We're brothers, best friends, an unstoppable force. The Redwood Rebels. Fuck with one, you fuck with us all.

Tommy claps his hands together to grab our attention. "Alright, so who called this little shindig by the fire? Sun's setting and I've got a hot guy waiting for me out front. Zed gave Jace a wedgie from hell just to make it happen, so let's get to it."

Talon downs his beer, then tosses the empty cup in the fire.

My eyes hold tight to the plastic and memories of the burning pictures flood my head. It was the last time we were standing together like this around a fire. All the secrets, lies, and deceit that we tossed into the fire that night, only to realize that no amount of flames can ever fully burn them.

Still watching the plastic slowly disintegrate, I stick my hands in my front pockets and speak, "I called us all together because I gave you my word. This has been a crazy fucking ride and I know that I'm the reason for all the extra stops and sharp turns. But, it all ends tonight." I look up, seeing Tommy across the fire, then Lars, and finally Talon—knowing that there's a good chance my best friends in the world will never speak to me again after this.

I have to do it, though. Every single thing I did from the moment I got that call from Vi was meant to protect her. Even if I didn't know it at the time—even if I just realized it a short time ago. Since the day she moved in next to me, she was under my protection. I was never the reaper after her soul, I was the soul-less boy after her heart. I was never gonna let her take the fall.

"It was me." I look around at each pair of eyes glowing back at me in the flame of the fire. "I hit Josh."

Everyone is silent. Even the blasting music up front and the chatter of the hundred guests has instantly diminished. It's just us and our held breaths, rapidly beating hearts, and the crackle of the fire in front of us.

No one says anything. So I take it upon myself to explain further. "Vi was never part of this. She was an innocent bystander who got caught up in a bad situation. She found proof that Josh was planning to kidnap Marni. I stumbled upon said proof and realized it was happening the next day. It came down to crunch time and he was ready to roll and make good on his plan, so I stopped him right before he had the chance. I hit him. Then I switched cars and grabbed my grandma's with every intention of picking his body up and throwing him off Miner Point."

More silence that has me really wishing I had another beer in my hand. I don't do awkward situations well, and this is really fucking awkward. "Would somebody say something? Damn."

"Six. Fucking. Months," Lars finally breaks the ice. "Six months and you've had us all walking on eggshells, digging, and searching, and this whole time it was you." He rounds the fire with his sights set on me and comes charging toward me. I jump to the side, right before he's ready to take me down, and he stumbles to catch his fall. "You're on a fucking roll. Josh and the pastor. Who's next?"

Now is probably a good time to tell them that credit isn't owed to me for that one. I assumed everyone thought it was me. I mean, Josh's body was in his basement and the box of pictures was next to his body. But, that was all on the pastor himself. Don't get me wrong, I would have done it. Was ready and willing, but he took matters into his own hands. My guess is, he realized his precious keepsake box was gone, then shot himself.

"Yeah, everyone keeps saying that, but I didn't kill the pastor."

Tommy holds up a hand, halting anyone from talking. "Wait a damn minute, you're telling me someone else killed that satanic bastard?"

"I'm telling you that I didn't do it. He shot himself right in front of me."

"One question." Lars holds up a finger, then brings it to his lips as he speaks, "What was your beef with the Bible hugger anyways? I mean, sure, it all came out after his death, but how'd you know about what he did?" His tone is sarcastic and forthcoming, and I realize that he doesn't suspect anything. He's asking out of sheer curiosity.

Pacing the length of the fire, I think. And think. And think. These are my boys and no matter what, I know I can trust them. We talk a lot of shit to each other, but they'd never judge me or turn on me. Vi is the only person I've ever said the words out loud to and I swore she'd be the only. But maybe I need to do this. Maybe this will help me heal.

Maybe it's time to bring the darkest part of my life into the light so that I can climb out of this black hole I've kept myself in for ten damn years.

"Well?" Lars asks.

Keeping my eyes on my feet, I dig my toe into the ground, kicking up tiny fragments of dirt and watching them fall carelessly back on my shoe. "Because my pictures were in that box, too."

There's so much silence that it's deafening. I hate the quiet. It makes me uneasy and unwell, especially when the focus is solely on me. They're all waiting for a reaction. If they expect me to break down, they've got another thing coming.

I've gotta get off this subject. They have the information they need. They can draw their own conclusions about how much of a fucked-up, broken person I am. "I understand that you're all pissed. I withheld some important information. But nothing's changed. In fact, I'm coming clean so we can all just move on from this shit. Don't you think it's high time?"

Tommy is the first to chime in, "Yes. Yes, I do. Thanks for telling us this. We still love ya, man. Yes, I'm really fucking pissed about the Josh shit. But, let's move on. It's a weight off all our shoulders."

Lars makes his way back over, taking a stance directly between me and the fire. Glaring at me, he responds to Tommy's suggestion. "I'll move on. But, I've got my eye on you. I'm sorry for what happened to you, but I know how you are with your games."

Throwing my hands up, I shrug. "No games. Just the truth."

"It shall set us free." Talon hoots with his cup up in the air. Pretty sure he's got no idea what's going on. If he were sober, he and I would likely be rolling in the fire this very second. "I say we all just finish off that keg and let Zed live his best life. After all, he was on the brink of death just last week."

Yep, he's definitely sloshed.

"Cheers to that. In fact, I'm gonna go grab myself a drink."

Now's a good time to make my exit. I can't handle the pity stares right now. I've gotta go talk to Marni. I've got one hour before I have to leave and I need to make my presence known to everyone here before I go.

I didn't plan on opening up like that, but nothing's changed. I won't let admitting it to them, or even myself, consume me for the next day, or year, or however long my fucked-up mind holds on to it this time.

Stammering bodies coat the walls of the building. Loud music blares, people are laughing and talking. Everyone is having a good time. I spot Marni by the keg with a swarm of drunkards around her and my eyes immediately shoot to a hand on her waist as she tries to slap it away.

"Go away!" she shrieks, but the guy doesn't take a fucking hint.

With two fingers between my teeth, I blow out my almighty ear-splitting whistle to grab the attention of the guys outside, then rip through the crowd to get to Marni. Grabbing the guy by the back of his shirt, I jerk him toward me. "Didn't she tell you to go away?" I swing him around and shove him up against the wall. My fingers wrap around his throat so tightly that I could end him in less than a minute if I wanted to, but I loosen my grip, saving that one for Talon.

I look over to Marni. "You okay?"

"Yeah, I'm fine. Just a dog barking up the wrong tree."

"What's this?" Lars asks as he and Tommy join my side. A herd has now gathered around us, watching and waiting for a show.

Talon staggers up slowly and places an arm around Marni's waist, then presses a kiss to her cheek with a smile, completely oblivious to the situation.

"This douchebag was groping Marni and wouldn't stop even when she told him to. What do we do with masochist douchebags, guys?"

Talon's eyes widen. "Is that true, babe?" When she nods, he

sees red. Practically jumping over the keg, he shoves me out of the way and takes my place in holding up the guy who fucked with the wrong girl. No one messes with one of our own. That now goes for Marni, Willa, Wyatt, and even Vi.

"I dunno, Zed. I kinda like to fuck with 'em a little bit." Lars whips out a switchblade, giving it a flick and opening it up. Everyone shrieks and takes a few steps back. Willa gives him an evil eye and shakes her head and his ego is instantly stomped on. He then folds that blade up and sticks it right back in his pocket. "Or, we could just kick him out."

"Come on, Lars," Willa says as she takes him by the hand. "I think it's time for us to go."

My eyes roll. "Dude, you are so fucking whipped," I mumble.

"Fuck off," Lars grumbles as he's pulled away.

Tommy takes a step toward the guy. "Well, at least show the girl what she was missing." In true Tommy fashion, instead of doing something heinous, he makes a mockery out of him by pulling his pants down.

Everyone laughs when his white briefs are exposed.

The guy clenches his thighs, trying to stop us from being able to pull his underwear down.

"Tell her you're sorry," Talon hisses through clenched teeth. I've gotta hand it to him. For being this shit-faced, his strength right now is impeccable.

"I'm sorry," the dude chokes out.

Now that I think of it, I've never seen this guy. Probably one of those college kids who crashes high school parties because he thinks it makes him look cool.

"Babe, anything you wanna do before I lower this jackass and toss him down the stairs out front."

Marni taps a finger to her chin. "Hmm," she walks over to him, observing his pale face, "maybe just this." She raises a hand and open-palm slaps him, sending the crowd into hysterics.

"Alright then." Talon releases his grip on the guy's neck and grabs him by the arm. Tommy follows behind as backup and I use this time to steal Marni away.

"Hey, you got a minute?" I ask her as she dusts her hands off with a grin on her face.

"I guess so." We walk side by side up the stairs and into the room the guys and I always use for our 'business.' "Thanks for doing that. I appreciate it."

"Yeah, no problem. Though I'm pretty sure you'd have no problem handling him yourself. You've got a killer right hook."

Marni laughs, and it's pacifying to the situation.

Once we're in the room, I leave the door open, even though there are people wandering the halls trying to scare themselves. Pretty sure I heard a few girls say they were looking for a ghost. I'd love to see their reaction when they actually find one, because they *are* in here.

"I'm sure Talon told you I called last night."

She nods, arms crossed over the chest of her Ravens hoodie. "He did."

"I'm just gonna lay it all out there. For starters, I'm sorry. I fucked up. A lot."

"Okay." She smiles. "Then let's just leave it at that. I appreciate that apology and I'd rather not rehash it all, so let's just move past it."

My brows hit my forehead. "Really?" That was way too easy.

"Yeah. Really. I forgive you, Zed. In fact, I forgave you a couple days ago when you opened up to the guys in Vi's driveway. It was really brave of you and it gave me good insight into how you've felt these past six months."

"Thanks, I guess." I don't really know what to say. What do you say to someone who forgives you for such a detestable thing?

"Ya know, Talon gives you a hard time, as you do to him, but he really does love you guys. All three of you. I'm gonna need you to keep on living because he needs you. We all do."

Fucking A, what is happening to me? Why does it feel like my heart is literally crying right now? Am I going through some sick hormonal change, because this can't be normal.

"Don't worry. I'm not going anywhere anytime soon. I've gotta stick around for a while. Someone has to keep these guys on their toes."

"Come on," she tips her head toward the door, "we better go make sure Talon isn't giving us six more months of hiding bodies and framing murderers."

"Yeahhhh, I think we've all had enough of that to last us awhile."

We go back downstairs and this weird feeling is still lingering. I actually feel relief. So much fucking relief.

I spot Tommy by the front door and approach him. "Hey, it's showtime."

He gives me a nod of approval before I turn around and inconspicuously go out the back door.

My job here is done. Now, it's time to close this pact and end this, once and for all.

CHAPTER TWENTY-TWO

Getting away with my mom and dad was everything I didn't know I needed. I truly believe that Mom is on a new path and trying to take in the beauty around her. She was kind, attentive, and pretty damn normal.

She's been planning this trip for a while. Apparently, Lake Havasu has a significance to her and she thought it was the perfect place to spread Josh's ashes. I bit my tongue the entire trip and felt a brush of relief as his ashes floated away. We were able to enjoy the remainder of the trip without his urn staring at me from the television stand in the hotel.

I may have cursed at him a few times, flipped it off once—then told him I was sorry for the way his life panned out. Josh was dealt a bad hand, but it doesn't change the fact that he was a monster with a mind that was as dangerous as a loaded gun.

Now, I'm home and have no idea where I go from here. Word has it, there's a big party at Briarwood tonight. There's no doubt that Zed is there. I'm sure he's back in with the guys and it's only a matter of time until his promise to me is voided.

He says he wants to protect me, but how can I truly believe

him when all he's ever done is hide me in the shadows and shun me to his friends?

Stretching my arm out, I roll over to my side and grab my phone. A new phone with no contacts. There are only a couple numbers I have memorized, and Zed's is one of them. The temptation to call him is real. I've fought it for two days, knowing that he couldn't reach me. Is he okay? Is he happy? Is he sad? God, I hope he's not sad.

My finger hovers over his name. It comes down, stops, goes back up. With a hefty sigh, I slam my phone on the bed. *No, I can't call him.*

I know he stopped by a couple times the day we left, so up until then, I know he's fine. I'm sure if something was wrong, I would have heard something from someone.

Just as the light of my phone diminishes beside me in my dark room, a loud crackle sound outside my window has me fleeing to the closed curtains. I tear them open and gasp when I see Zed's house completely engulfed in flames.

I stare at it, stuck in a trance and mesmerized by the glow.

"Mom!" I scream at the top of my lungs as I try to pull myself together. I grab my phone off the bed and dial 911. "Mom!" I scream again. The operator picks up immediately.

I spit out the words in one breath, "Hurry, there's a fire. A house. The address is 9436 Sapphire Lane." I end the call and dial Zed, but it goes straight to his voicemail.

"Shit!" My foot stomps the floor. I peel my eyes off the blaze and hurry downstairs.

"Mom," I shout one last time.

Mom lifts her head from the kitchen counter, where she's flipping through a magazine. "My God, Vi. What is all the yelling for?"

I push past her and walk hurriedly through the kitchen. "The neighbor's house is on fire. I called 911, but I have to go make sure he's not in there, Mom." Tears prick my eyes and my chest holds the weight of an elephant. "He can't be. He can't be in there." I break down before hauling ass out the back door.

Mom chases after me, hollering words that I don't even comprehend as I approach Zed's house. Heat pours off it, feeling as though my skin is melting just from the smoke alone. "Zed!" I scream at the top of my lungs. In doing so, I fill them up with a cloud of black smoke that sends me into a coughing fit.

Please don't let him be in here.

"Zed!"

I get closer as ash and embers fall toward me. Lifting up the hood of my sweatshirt, I grip it tightly, holding it out to stop anything from hitting my face.

"Vienna, don't you dare. You stop right now," Mom bellows. I can feel her arms wrap around me, trying to pull me back, but I fight her off, kicking and screaming.

"I have to make sure he's not inside," I cry out. "I can't live without him, Mom." I give her a shove, then take off running to the back of Zed's house. The glass doors have been shattered, but there's a small opening.

Sirens sound in the distance, but I can't wait. He could be unconscious at this point. He could be... No! I won't think like that.

Without any hesitation, I hold my hood out over my head, shielding my face, and run in the back door. "Zed! Please, if you're in here, answer me." I cough a few times, clearing my lungs.

Mom's cries ring out from the doorway, but I pay her no attention.

I look all around the kitchen, watching as it slowly catches fire and spreads inch by inch. Orange and yellow hued balls of ardent flames advance through the entire room. There's a loud thud that sends my heart into a frenzy, and my eyes widen as a black cloud of smoke suddenly swarms me.

I cough, trying to rid my lungs of the smoke. But no matter how hard I try, I can't get it out.

It hurts. I go to turn back, feeling defeated, but my feet fail me. My body fails me.

I can't speak; I can't catch my breath. I can't breathe.

CHAPTER TWENTY-THREE

ZED

Flashing lights and sirens flood the streets of Redwood. Some turning left, others turning right.

Two major fires at two different locations.

Such a shame.

With a permagrin painted on my face, I head out of town and back toward the party.

The party is still going strong when I pull up; in fact, there seems to be even more people here than when I left. The bass coming from two large speakers placed out front can be felt through the seat of my truck as I come to a stop.

It's only been an hour and a half since I left, but half of the crowd looks inebriated. I close my truck door and make my way over to a new keg that sits outside. Right beside it is Tommy. Beside him, Wyatt.

Lars and Willa left. Talon and Marni probably weren't far behind, considering Talon could barely hold his own weight on his feet.

"Yo, Zed," Tommy calls out from a distance.

I keep on my path toward him, but I'm stopped when a girl jumps out in front of me. She's got streaks of liquid spilled down the front of her shirt, her eyes are only half-open, and she reeks of vomit. "Hey, you." She pokes a finger into my chest.

She looks familiar, but I can't remember where I've seen her before.

"You picked me up earlier and I did not like that." Her words stutter out as she struggles to even form a sentence. "You're a bad boy. I can tell."

I look past her, trying to grab Tommy's attention to come rescue me from this shit-faced chick. Really don't wanna have to be mean to her, but I will if she doesn't get the fuck out of my way.

"Yeah, well, next time maybe you should just keep your mouth shut." Looking over her shoulder again, I wave Tommy down. My hand lingers over her head and I point at her. "Little help here."

"I happen to like bad boys, ya know."

Fuck my life.

"I'm sure you do, but I'm not the bad boy for you. Now, if you don't mind, I've got shit to do." I go to walk past her, but her boisterous friends join our side.

"I remember you, Mr. Tough Guy." She holds out her camera like she's taking pictures and I use this opportunity to my advantage and let her snap a few shots with the partygoers in the background. Some minors getting busted for drinking sure as hell beats a life sentence for arson.

"Might wanna get your friend home. She's toast," I tell the photographer chick before leaving them.

I'm finally free of them, but I can feel their eyes on the back of my head. "That girl needs to go take a fucking nap," I tell Tommy, who's now hoisting someone up by her waist over the keg. Her legs stick straight in the air as Wyatt holds the nozzle to her mouth and everyone chants for her to chug.

Really wish I wouldn't have come back here. Parties have never been a fun scene for me. I'm not really a people person and this party is an introvert's worst nightmare.

"Did you do what you had to do?" Tommy sets the girl down and pulls me to the side of the crowd. "Heard a bunch of sirens. I sure as hell hope you covered your tracks, whatever it was."

"No worries. Everything is fine. I'll probably hang for a few, then..." My words drag off as my phone begins vibrating in my pocket. I take a look at the caller ID and smirk. "I've gotta take this." I walk away and keep walking until the noise is no longer threatening to rupture my eardrum. I tap *Answer* and take the call. "Thought I might hear from you eventually," I say into the speaker of the phone.

"You think you're smooth, don't ya?" Dad screeches. "You really fucked up this time, son."

"I don't know what you're talking about. I'm at a party with my friends. Celebrating spring break. You must be confused." I keep walking with one hand in my pocket and that grin still painted on my face.

"Hey, I'm not complaining much. I'll get me a pretty little insurance policy that'll set me up somewhere nice away from this trash town and that hellhole business your mom started up for me. I just hope you have a solid alibi. If that neighbor girl dies, you're gonna need it."

My feet stop. Pretty sure my heart stopped, too. "What are you talking about?"

"Oh," he blows air. "You didn't know? The girl next door was found in our kitchen. Wasn't breathing when paramedics arrived. I'm to assume that wasn't part of your diabolical plan?"

My phone falls from my hand, rolling off my shoe and landing face up on the ground. "No," I mutter, shaking my head in disbelief. It can't be Vi. There's no way she was in the house. I was there. She wasn't.

Everything was planned perfectly. I killed the cameras, poured the gasoline, struck the match, lit the candle and put a piece of paper on it, then ran like hell out the side door of the garage. Vi wasn't there. I would have seen her.

My heart resumes beating at an alarming rate.

Bending down, I grab my phone, end the call, and run like hell. The word 'no' on repeat in my head.

Shoving everyone out of the way, I don't stop. "Fucking move!" I scream as I barrel through the crowd.

∞

I'M NOT SURE HOW, or even when, I ended up in Vi's driveway, next to my old house that is now a pile of sweltering rubble with only the backside intact. Dad stands out front with a uniformed police officer and a fireman. He points at me, but I don't give it a second thought as I go straight to Vi's front door.

My mind is a haze and I'm unable to put together even the simplest thought. All I can focus on is Vi.

Pounding my fist to the door continuously, I shout, "Open the door!" *Pound. Pound. Pound.* "Open the damn door."

When no one answers, I jump off the steps and run over to Dad, who's still standing there engaged in a conversation with the officer. "Where the hell is she?" I say to him with my eyes locked on his.

"She was taken to Mercy Hospital in Wausau," Dad tells me.

There's a very good chance he's in the process of pinning this on me right now, but fuck it. I don't even care. I have to get to the hospital and make sure she's okay.

I turn to walk away, but Dad grabs me by the arm. Jerking it away, I hiss, "I don't have time for this shit."

He comes closer and whispers, "I'm not telling them my suspicions, but you better hope like hell that girl lives. If this turns into a manslaughter investigation, you will get caught."

"I didn't do this," I spit out the cold, hard lie.

Wanting like hell to believe it myself. Wishing it were true. Because if I didn't do this, it never would have happened.

If she dies, I'm going with her. I can't live in this world

without her in it. She's the only person who makes it worth living at all.

∞

FORTY-FIVE MINUTES LATER, I'm walking briskly through the halls of the hospital. I've never been a fan of hospitals. So much sickness and death. Some heal, some don't. The smell alone makes me nauseous, and adding that to my anxious state, it's taking everything in me to swallow down the bile rising in my throat.

My hands slam on the receptionist's desk, grabbing the lady's attention. She pushes her glasses up on her head and sneers at me. "May I help you?"

"Vienna Moran. I need her room number."

After a few taps of the keyboard, she points me in the direction of Vi. "Down the hall, take the first set of elevators to the second floor. She's in ICU room 280. I doubt she's allowed—"

I don't even let her finish before my sneakers are squeaking across the marbled floors to the elevators.

My finger taps repeatedly at the arrow pointed up until the elevator stops and the doors slide open. An elderly couple make their way out at a very, very, very slow pace. I step to the side and try to refrain from an outburst. They're actually pretty fucking sweet, the way the old man is helping her out. Her frail arm can barely lift her cane over the gap in the doorway. He bends over, almost throwing his back out, and lifts the end of her cane until it's finally on solid ground. I press my hand to the sliding door, keeping it open for them, while I wait, very impatiently.

"Thank you, young man," the gentleman says.

I nod with a smile, then take one large step into the elevator. Hitting the close button over and over again until the doors finally shut.

Once it comes to a stop, I jump out and begin searching for

room 280. Not needing to look any further, I spot Vi's mom and dad.

They're standing outside her room. Mrs. Moran's face is buried into Mr. Moran's shoulder. Why is she crying so hysterically? Why are they standing out here instead of being in there with their daughter?

No.

Without a word, I slowly approach them. When Mr. Moran acknowledges me and pats his wife's shoulder, she turns around. No one says anything.

My legs begin to feel weak. My body off-balance.

"Is she...?" I can't say the word. I'm not sure what word I was looking for. Okay? Hurt? Dead?

"Oh, Zed," Mrs. Moran says, pulling me in for a hug. Something must be very wrong. Mrs. Moran hates my guts. Even if she did tell me when Vi went to Vegas, it took a lot of persuasion.

"How did she get into my house? When? Why?" I finally speak. Getting all the questions out at once.

"She was looking for you, Zed. She was worried you were inside. I tried to stop her, but she wasn't having it."

"No," I say again. At least I think I said it. Maybe it was just in my head. After all, it's been on repeat in my mind. "Why the hell would she do that?"

Mrs. Moran takes a step back. "Isn't it obvious? She loves you."

There's an unusual pang in my chest. It hurts more than anything I've ever felt before. Worse than the burning touch of the pastor. Worse than the feeling I had the day Mom died. Worse than saying goodbye to Vi two years ago. It's even worse than passing her in the halls at school, knowing she was so close, yet so far away.

Vi does love me. She's always loved me.

"She'll be okay, right?" I ask, feeling like my entire life is hanging on the answer to that one question.

"She's going to be fine."

I breathe out a hefty sigh of relief. "I need to see her. Can I... see her?"

Mr. Moran speaks in a gruff voice. "The doctor is with her right now. She just had some tests and she's getting examined. Once he comes out, we'll let you go in."

I give him a nod, run my fingers through my hair, and press my back to the wall of the long stretch of hallway. And I wait.

Five minutes later, the handle on the door turns and I push myself off the wall. The doctor comes out and I don't even wait for him to say anything before I slither through the opening and go inside.

The first sight of her has me pinching the bridge of my nose, stopping any tears that threaten to break through. I haven't cried since I was a kid. But this is really hard to see.

Vi lies there on that bed with her eyes shut and a tube in each of her nostrils. An IV is attached and pumping fluids into her. A blood pressure cuff begins inflating around her tiny arm. And her perfect toes slightly wiggle before her eyes flutter and open.

She looks over at me, taking a minute to realize who's standing at the side of her bed. "Zed," she says with hoarseness in her voice. "What...what are you doing here?"

I take her delicate hand in mine, the same one that has the tube running to her wrist. I turn it over and look at her palm, tracing lines up each of her fingers to distract myself because if I look into her eyes right now, I'm gonna fucking break down, and I refuse to do it. "You really need to quit trying to save me." I choke out the words around the lump stuck in my throat. I swallow hard, lift my head, and look at her.

She retorts with a wounded smile. "You really need to quit scaring me." Tears follow her words, sliding shamelessly down her rosy-red cheeks.

"Please, don't cry," I beg her, sweeping my thumb under one eye, then the next.

"I was so…" She's cut off by a coughing fit. A very coarse bark that sounds like sandpaper ripping through her airways. "I was so scared."

I shake my head. "Don't. We can talk about it later. Just rest." I take a seat on the edge of the bed, still holding her hand. Her eyes fight to stay open, so I just sit here quietly, watching, waiting, and wondering.

She's in this hospital because of me. The exact reason I stayed away from her all these years, yet here she is. Hurt, because of me. Everything I touch breaks. Everything I love dies.

Maybe it was smart to keep my distance. But what is this life without her by my side? I'm not sure I know anymore.

Ever since she pulled me off that ledge, she's lived in my thoughts. It's like the two years in between never happened and my heart was beating with purpose again.

She's my purpose. She's my reason to live.

But at what cost? What will I do next that puts her in the hospital or six feet in the ground? Can I really protect her when I'm the very person she needs protection from?

Minutes pass until the doors slowly open and her parents come inside. Vi is sound asleep so I gently set her hand down and step away to hear what they have to say.

Mrs. Moran whispers, "Her X-rays were good. There's no lung damage. Her oxygen is still a bit low and her carbon monoxide levels are a tad high. She'll likely sleep on and off due to the high levels, but once those are normal, we get to take her home."

"That's good news," I exhale deeply. "Can I stay with her until she goes home?"

Her parents share a look, then Mrs. Moran nods. "Her dad is going home for the night. I'll be staying. I'll probably try to get some sleep on the couch in here, but I can have the nurse bring in a chair for you."

"No. That's okay. I'll just stand."

"Are you sure?"

"Positive."

Mr. Moran says his goodbyes and her mom gets comfortable on the couch while I sit on the edge of the bed, watching Vi sleep peacefully.

I've always thought that my life was in shambles because of everything I've been through, but Vi has been through just as much, if not more. She may have ran out of fear for her future, but every time she fell down, she picked herself back up. If I had to choose one person that I admire most in the world, I think it'd be her. She's the epitome of a fighter.

I'll never forget the first time I saw her when she moved in next door. The second time I saw her was at church. Her family had just moved to town and she was this firecracker who refused to sit still during the service. The pastor recommended some one-on-one time with her to get her acquainted with the fellowship. He claimed to be personable and wanted to form special relationships, with not only the adults of his church, but also their children. Eventually, she was brought into his disciples' class on Wednesday nights.

At that time, there were only four of us. As we grew, new kids joined. Eventually, the classes stopped, but I'm not sure he ever did.

I remember looking into her eyes and her looking into mine. I wanted to kill him right then with my bare hands. Thought about it, too. I swore one day I'd do it. I'd kill him for what he did.

I got close.

"I don't like this place, Zed. It gives me the creeps."

I huff. "You and me both."

"Beats the stench on the ride here that rolled from the trunk."

Vi had her face in her shirt the entire drive. At one point, I thought for sure we'd have to pull over so she could throw up. But she held it together.

"I told you that I'd do this alone. You shouldn't even be here."

"Umm, yes, I should. I want this son of a bitch to pay just as much as you do."

With the box gripped tightly in one hand and my other on the gun stuffed in the waistband of my jeans, I kick open the screen door. A flicker of light shines through the room from the muted television.

Rick springs up from his chair, a newspaper falling weightlessly to the carpet. The chair continues to rock although his body has left it. He takes one look at me, then the box, and hauls ass out of the room.

"Not so fast." I charge after him, dropping the box from my hand, the pictures scattering around on the floor of the hallway. I pull the gun from my waistband, still following hurriedly behind him. He runs into his room and pulls open the top drawer of a dresser. "Stop right there." Pointing the gun at the back of his head, I step closer.

Vi comes out of nowhere with the box.

"Get out of here," I shout to her. "You don't wanna see this."

In a moment of weakness, I turn to look at Vi for clarity. That one brief moment stole my destiny from me.

Pastor Jeffries turns to look at me. His own gun now perched in the palm of his hand. His arm rises in slow motion as the barrel presses to his temple.

"Close your eyes, Vi!" I scream as his finger presses down on the trigger. Blood squirts out the side of his head, splattering across the wall with fragments of brain tissue dropping aimlessly onto the white sheets of his bed. His knees hit the floor first, his eyes glued to mine as all life leaves them. Then, his entire weight drops with a thud.

"No," I cry out in anger. "I was supposed to do it. It was my retribution." I drop to my knees in front of his lifeless body.

"We've gotta go, Zed." Vi tries frantically to pull me up. "Hurry, we've gotta go now."

Once I'm able to tear my eyes from him, the anger settling into something worse—misery—I grab the box from Vi. "Are you sure there aren't any of us in here?"

"I checked three times. We got them all."

I slide the box over beside the soulless body, hoping that whatever lived inside of him is spending an eternity burning in hell.

It was supposed to be my one shot—a bullet in his head, from my gun. He stole it from me.

He's gone, nonetheless, and it's time for Vi and me to try and let go of what this fucker did to us.

Vi begins stirring, snapping me out of the trance I fell into. "Hey," I say when her eyes dawn on me. "How you feeling?"

She shifts into a sitting position, so I grab the bedside remote and raise the top of it to make her more comfortable.

"Thirsty." She smacks her lips together. "Really thirsty."

I grab a lidded Styrofoam cup off the bed tray and shake it, but it's empty.

"Just press that nurse button on the remote," she tells me.

I press it, but seconds later, no one comes. "Want me to go get some water? Or grab the nurse?"

"No, that's okay. They'll come."

"Well, good news is, I think you'll be getting out of this place soon."

After a few minutes of small talk, the nurse still hasn't come. Vi begins coughing again, and her lips are dry as fuck. So I take it upon myself to get her some water, since these damn people don't know how to do their jobs.

"Be right back," I tell her.

"Where are you going?"

Without responding, I pull open the door to the hallway. When I see three nurses hovering over a phone and laughing at something they find funny, my blood boils. "Whose job do I need to threaten to get some damn service?"

All eyes shoot to me, but no one moves.

I pull the door closed behind me and walk toward them. "You," I point to the nurse who was in earlier, "your patient rang you five minutes ago and she needs some water. Either you get it now or I'll be having a word with you supervisor."

The nurse swipes out of whatever was on her phone, looks at the girls, who are just as stunned as she is, then steps out from behind the desk. "I'll get that for her now."

I go back to Vi's room and she's sporting a scowl meant just for me. "Was that really necessary?"

"Do you have your water yet?"

"Well, no, but—"

"Then yes, it was necessary."

I look over at her mom who's wide awake now and grinning from ear to ear, pleased with my bold personality.

Only seconds later, the nurse comes in with a fresh cup of water. She doesn't even look at me, just goes straight to Vi and hands it to her. "I apologize for the wait. We've been swamped."

"Yeah, with TikTok videos," I mutter under my breath.

Completely ignoring me, she continues, "I've just got word that the doctor is making rounds and as long as your levels are looking good, you'll be getting released. I'll get started on your release papers now."

Finally, we can blow this joint. I have so much I need to say to Vi, but not in this hospital, and not with her mom five feet away.

I need to tell her about last night and how it was all my fault. How do you tell someone they almost died because of you?

CHAPTER TWENTY-FOUR

Zed met me at the front door of Mom's car when we got home. He helped me in the house, took off my shoes, yelled at the gardener who he thought left a shovel in the path to the front door. I didn't tell him it was my mom who suddenly grew a green thumb.

Then, he helped me up to my room where a bouquet of sunflowers were waiting for me.

Who is this guy?

"You don't have to do all of this," I tell Zed as he fluffs out the pillows on my bed. "I seriously feel completely normal. Just a little cough, but I'm okay."

"You need to rest."

"No," I say in a stark response, "I need food."

"You're hungry? What do you want?" His hand digs into the front pocket of his jeans and he pulls out his phone. "I'll order from Scotty's and go pick it up."

I grab his arm and pull him down on the bed until he's sitting next to me. My legs cross, and I take his hands in mine. "Would you just stop for a minute and talk to me? What the hell happened last night?"

Zed blinks a few times, squeezes my hands, looks at them, looks at the ceiling—does everything but answer my question.

I push further, "Well, do you plan on telling me?"

As he gets to his feet, he starts pacing. "I started the fire. I took back what he stole from my mom, let him keep his house and his business, then I lit both places on fire. First the house, then King Corp. You almost died because of me."

"Zed," I grab his arm and pull him down, though he refuses to look me in the eye, "look at me." I cup his cheeks in my hands. "I went into that house of my own free will. I went in because I thought you were inside. But you weren't, and I'm here. Alive. Don't drive yourself crazy with what-ifs, just let it go."

"If you had died because—"

"I didn't. So stop."

He finally looks me in the eye. His are warm and soft, but hold a dejection in them that I want to erase. "So, what now?"

What now? That's a good question. When I don't respond right away, he straightens his back and looks away. Slow steps lead him over to a corkboard I have on the wall that's covered in old gothic magazine clippings. His fingers graze the bottom of each one as he takes them in, though he's seen them before.

"Are you staying in Redwood, or going back to Vegas?" he asks, prying further for an answer to his question.

My plan was to go back, but how will he react to that?

"I'm not really sure yet. I was thinking of at least going to stay with my aunt for a while. A couple months maybe? Get a job, finish out the school year online." Zed might be done with school, because he never finished, but I still have a year left. While I have no intention of finishing it out on campus, I do plan to finish.

Hands dropping to his sides, he spins around to face me. "So, you're leaving me again?"

"You don't have to look at it like that. Besides, dead-end, remember?" I stand up and walk toward him, hoping to calm him down before he gets upset. I know he wants me to stay, but he doesn't seem to grasp that I can't. I go to reach for him, but he takes a step back.

"God, you're so infuriating. So beautifully, fucking infuriating." His arms descend toward me, but stop in midair. Fists clenched, knuckles white. He shrieks while racking his brain for his next move. A grueling expression and a tortured mind. It's like he wants to grab me, but not in a painful way. "Damnit, Vi. I fucking love you. Only you. The whole world could go up in flames, but I'd die trying to carry you out of it." He takes another step back, slowly dropping to his knees in front of me. "I'm beyond repair, but I wanna be better, even if it's only for you." His face falls in his hands, while I melt into a puddle of goo right before him.

Did he really just tell me he loves me?

"You love me?" I choke out the words, low and desolate.

Zed raises his head, looking into my eyes, and that's when I see the vulnerability I've been searching for, for three whole years. "Is that enough?" he asks.

"It's…it's everything." Dropping down in front of him, my eyes level with his. Like Zed, I'm terrible with words and emotions—not quite as terrible as Zed is—but, this push and pull between us has gone on long enough. I'm at the point where we are either all in, or I'm out.

"I love you, too. All your flaws, all your demons, and all of your perfect imperfections. I've always loved you. Since the first time I saw you, I felt an out-of-this-world connection with you. It was like I always knew our worlds were meant to collide. Whether we're together or we're not, you'll always be my soulmate."

He bites back a smile, while I do the same. Instead of responding with words, he presses his lips to mine. His sweet lips that know how to find mine even in the darkness. I drop back on the floor, his body cloaking mine, and I wrap my arms around him, never wanting to let go.

He just confessed his love to me, while I did the same, but so many questions are left unanswered. I want to trust him. I want to let him love me and love him right back, but I have to know what he plans to do with the knowledge he has. I can't just forget about the phone call I heard. He told them they'd get what they want. What they want is me.

Pulling back, I break the kiss. "So, what's changed? Why now?" It sounded better in my head, but I need to know.

"Does there have to be a reason? You almost died because of me—for me. Because you left me in Vegas, and because you keep leaving me. And because, I want you to stay in Redwood...with me."

My eyes close, my chin hitting my sternum. "I get it," I whisper. "You want me to come back with you so that you can," I air quote, "get what you want from the guys?" I'm such a fool. This is all an act and I should have seen it coming.

"No, Vi. The minute you walked back into my life, for the third time, I knew that I couldn't let you walk back out of it. The thing with the guys is over. You don't have to worry about them anymore."

"How can you be so sure?"

"Last night, I confessed to them. Told them it was me that hit Josh."

My eyes widen. "You what? No." I shake my head. "Please tell me you did not do that."

"I did."

"Why the hell would you tell them that, Zed?" I slap his arm but want to hug him at the same time.

"It was the right thing to do. I know these guys better than anyone and them thinking that I killed Josh was the only way to get them to back off. They'd drive themselves mad trying to solve that death. Well, now it's solved. We can all move on from this."

His shoulders rise and fall. "It's what we do. I save you, and you save me."

"Yeah. Yeah, I guess we do." I smile back at him, truly, madly in love with this guy.

I can't believe he did this for me. I'm speechless, yet so grateful. I really shouldn't be this surprised; Zed swore he'd always protect me, and he's proving to be a man of his word.

∞

ZED LEFT to go get food, so I use this opportunity to take a shower and rid myself of the ash and smoke caked in my hair. I smell like a chimney and still have soot on parts of my body.

As per usual, I crank the shower to as hot as I can get it, without stripping the skin off my bones. I step in, letting the water fall unsparingly on my dry skin.

My heart feels so full right now. Zed said the words I've always wanted to hear, and I feel as though I'm in a dream that I never want to wake from.

I still can't believe he told the guys he killed Josh. While I wish he wouldn't have done that, it certainly makes things easier for me. I suppose I should call Adaline and let her know that we don't have to worry about this anymore.

After all, she was part of this, too.

Adaline came up with the idea to drug Josh to stop him until we came up with another plan. We were running out of time and it was a last-minute decision. We got the drugs in him, but before we could get to him, he ended up driving his car and parking it down the road from Marni's. He was really fucked-up and unpredictable. There was no doubt his intentions were depraved.

I was driving really fucking fast to try to stop him. Adaline was in the passenger seat, her wheelchair folded up in the back.

"What do I do?" I scream with tears streaming down my face.

"Hit him. You have to. Just fucking hit him."

I come closer and closer, my fingers wrapped so tightly around the steering wheel that all the blood has drained from my hands.

"I can't!" I cry out, but my words are muffled by Adaline's screams.

"Do it! Just hit him. He's a monster, Vi. He's a fucking monster."

My foot slams down on the gas, my eyes zeroed in on him. Catching sight of the headlights, he turns and looks right at me with wide and fearful eyes. But I swear to God I see him fucking smile through it when I run right over his ass.

I don't stop. I keep going, never looking back.

Silence engulfs us for a half-mile until I finally whip off to the side of the road. Then, I pull out my phone and don't even seek Adaline's approval for my next move. I'm too stunned to even think. My hands tremble as I try to press the name on my contact list.

He picks up on the first ring. Through the sniffles and heady breaths, I manage to choke out the words. "Zed, I need your help. I just killed my brother."

There's only a brief pause before he asks," Where?"

"Right in front of Marni Thorn's house. He was gonna—"

"Go home. Don't tell a fucking soul."

He ends the call.

Adaline looks at me with displeasure, but I assure her, "It's okay. We can trust him."

I was right all along, even when I wasn't sure. Zed might wear this scary mask, but deep down, he's just a broken boy with a wounded heart.

Just like he wants to protect me, I plan on protecting him. If those guys give him any shit, I'll have no problem putting them in their place and reminding them of everything Zed did to help them.

CHAPTER TWENTY-FIVE

ZED

A week has passed since Vi was released from the hospital. That's one week that neither of us have felt the need to look over our shoulders and wonder who or what may hold our fate in their hands.

I've been staying at the inn, getting snide looks from Mrs. Mayberry each time I come or go, which is often, considering I'm at Vi's house all day. Her parents have been surprisingly accepting, though they won't let me spend the night.

The future is still full of so much uncertainty. I'm currently homeless with a nine-figure bank account. Vi is still unsure about staying in Redwood, and I don't really blame her. We've got friends here, and her family, but other than that, the town holds too many terrible memories. I'm all for getting the hell out of here.

"Finished," Vi says as she slaps her laptop closed.

"Bring on summer vacay," I hoot. It's not really summer, but Vi finished up her online classes for the year and she's officially a senior now.

Giving her laptop a push to the side, I grab her by the waist and pull her on top of me. Our stomachs mesh together and her face lingers over mine. "And now for the age-old question, what's next?"

"Hmm," she taps a finger to her chin with a devilish little smirk, "I can think of a couple things."

"I like the way you think, but while a rebel and all, I'm not too keen on fucking you under your dad's roof."

"You're no fun." She twists her smile and pouts. "I wish we were back in Nanjunction."

Furrowing my brows, I look at her with a crooked grin. "Really? You liked that place?"

"I loved it. It was so peaceful and quiet. I could seriously see myself living there one day."

"Thought you wanted to be a city girl?"

"People change."

My head drops down on the pillow as my fingers tease the small of her back in featherlike strokes, leaving a trail of goosebumps in their path. "It's two hours away. Doubt your parents would ever let that fly."

"Doesn't matter what they say. I'm eighteen years old. I might still have a year left of school, but I can live wherever I want as long as I finish. Besides, Mom was all for me living in Vegas. It's fucking Sin City. I'm sure they'd be agreeable to seeing me live somewhere that I won't be surrounded by sex and sin."

"Who says you wouldn't be surrounded by that in the Nano house? I happen to be full of sin that I have every intention of pumping into you through sexual acts."

Her cheeks blush and it makes me smile. "And I'm not opposed to that at all." She leans forward and kisses my lips. "But, apparently you are."

"We can leave this house right now. I'll fuck you on the hood of your car down the road. As long as we're not on your parents' property, I'll gladly dive into this." I slap a hand to her tight ass.

"Let's do it."

"Go down the road and fuck? Hell yeah." I shift her body and go to stand up.

"No," she chuckles, pushing me back down, "let's go back to Nanjunction. Even if it's just for a week."

"I mean, I sort of have a lot going on, but I think I can squeeze in a week at a remote house in the wilderness with a smoking hot chick." It's a lie and she knows it. I have nothing going on. No job, no schooling, not a damn thing. I'm actually a big fucking loser right now.

"Really?" Her eyes light up with excitement.

"Sure. Why not?"

Vi jumps off the bed and immediately grabs a duffle bag and starts stuffing clothes in it like she's filling a bag for a dollar at a yard sale. "Whoa, we've got the rest of our lives. Chill out."

I climb off the bed and walk over to her, wrapping my arms around her waist from behind. "I wanna do something before we go." My face nuzzles into the nape of her neck, and she lets out a subtle moan when I suck in the delicate skin.

"I thought you said not in the house."

"Not that. I wanna take you somewhere."

∞

AFTER A QUICK CALL to the guys, I've assembled them for a meeting. Everyone is at Talon's house and for the first time since Halloween, I'm pulling up feeling like I'm not the outcast. We haven't talked much since the party, but they know what went down.

The fires, Vi.

"I don't know about this," Vi says nervously from the passenger seat of my truck. "They all hate me. After what I did to Willa and then running away, making myself look guilty as hell."

"Listen, babe," I squeeze her inner thigh, "these guys have done so much worse than you. There's not a person in that house who hasn't made a move to protect their own ass. Once you get to know them, you'll see they're not as bad as the picture everyone's painted."

"Including you?"

I suppose I have painted them in a bad light, but it was all just a shitload of miscommunication, bad choices, and wrong turns. "Even me."

We get out of the truck and I throw an arm around Vi's shoulder. I settle a cigarette behind my ear, hoping I won't need it. I know these guys will be accepting of Vi, but if they say one wrong thing and I have to take someone down, I'll need a smoke after.

Not even bothering to knock, I walk right in. Vi presses her side firmly against mine and squeezes my waist. She's nervous, naturally. It's been a wild and bumpy ride. She ran from these guys for months—trying to throw shades of suspicion elsewhere.

"What's up, boys?" I tip my chin up, then look down at Vi. "You all know Vi?"

Tommy smiles, waves, and then returns to shading a tree on the side of a cardboard box. He's always found art in the strangest of places.

"Hey, Vi," Willa says, with her normal sweet tone. "Come on in. Have a seat." She pats the cushion beside her and I think it helps to calm Vi's nerves a little bit.

Vi did go on the news and claim that she thought Willa and Josh ran off together. Willa confronted her, and Vi told her she thought they had. To Willa, it's the truth. Vi was no part of Josh's death as far as everyone knows.

Marni and Talon come walking in the room. Talon adjusts his zipper on his jeans, wearing a shit-eating grin, and there's no doubt about what they were just doing. His fingers weave through his bedhead hair. "Hey, man." He drops down on the couch next to Marni.

I walk farther into the room and Willa is now showing Vi

pictures from her latest ultrasound. "How much longer?" I ask Willa.

"Six very long weeks," she says with a drawn-out sigh.

"So, what's up? You two just come to hang out or what?" Lars speaks up with a toothpick stuck between his teeth.

"Pretty much. Came to tell you guys that me and Vi are heading to Nanjunction for a week or two."

"Nanjunction? What the hell does that town have that you want?" Tommy laughs, without taking his eyes off his artwork.

"Absolutely nothing. That's what we like it about."

Talon twists his head to look at me while I stand beside Vi on the couch. "Well, we were about to throw some burgers on the grill. Drink some beer. Play some horseshoes. You two down?"

Vi looks up at me. "That sounds fun."

I shrug. "Sure. Why the hell not."

This feels normal. Like old times. It feels really fucking good.

And to think I might have missed this if Vi hadn't shown up at Rubble Edge at the exact time she did.

CHAPTER TWENTY-SIX

ZED

"Why are you acting so weird?" Vi laughs with her eyes hidden beneath the mask I put over them. "It's not like I don't know where we're going."

"Would you just relax and let me give you this one surprise?"

I shift into park and hop out, hurrying over to her side, so I can open the door before she does. It'd be just our luck, she'd miss the step and fall on her face. We're both prone to fucking things up significantly. Lifting her by the waist, I set her down then take her hand, leading her over to the front of the house. Once I have her positioned just right, I step behind her, remove the blindfold, and let her have a look.

My chin presses to her shoulder. "What do you think?"

"Aww, you filled the bird feeder." She turns around and throws her arms around my neck.

I knew that's the first thing she would see. I spin her back around. "Look again."

It takes her a minute, but when she faces me again with a dropped jaw, I know she saw the 'sold' sign in the yard.

"No way! You bought this place?"

"Yep. It's all ours."

She quirks a brow. "Was it even for sale?"

"No. But I made a generous offer to the owner and he accepted. You said you liked it here. I figured, why not buy it and make it our own. I'm not a fan of the linen closet being in the hall, or the—"

She cuts me off by smashing her lips to mine. So hard that I'm pretty positive her lip ring just busted me open. "I love you," she mutters into my mouth.

"Love you, too, babe." I pull back and look into the eyes I want to look into for the rest of my life. "And you know what this means? We don't have to fuck on the hood of your car on the road now. This place is ours and we can do whatever the hell we want." I scoop my hands under her ass and lift her up. Her legs wrap around me. With the truck door still wide open, I carry her up to the house—our house.

The moment is perfect, everything about it. Our lips cement together, my cock is throbbing and ready to go. Then we reach the door. I go to open it and it's locked. "Shit."

"What's wrong?" Her legs slide down and she stands up.

I pat my pockets, look over at the truck, and back to her. "I don't have a key." *Fuck!* I left the damn key in the hotel in Redwood. "Son of a bitch!" Vi laughs as if it's just the funniest thing ever. "How is this funny?"

"Because it's so us." She looks around the house and then she gets that look on her face. The one where I know her wheels are spinning. Her body slides up against mine, she peers up at me and kisses my chin. "How bad do you want me right now?"

My teeth graze my lip, biting at the corner. "Is that even a question?"

"Then take me. Right here and now. We're on private property. No neighbors for miles."

I like the way she thinks. Vi is my kind of crazy. "Right here? On this porch?"

"Porch, grass, truck—doesn't matter to me."

It feels like it's been an eternity since I've been inside her and I'd be willing to fuck her just about anywhere. I'm just really pissed that we have this entire house and we're locked out of it.

Before I can say anything, she lifts her shirt over her head. The silky skin of her cleavage peeks out at me from her bra. Tempting, seductive, and so damn inviting. She licks her lips, and I catch myself licking mine back.

With one hand, I grab her by the waist and pull her chest to mine. "Mmm," I hum. "So fucking gorgeous."

As she looks deep into my eyes, her hands begin working their magic. First unbuttoning my jeans, then sliding my pants down. Her fingers wrap around my rock-hard cock, stroking back and forth.

"So, right here?" I ask, being sure that this is, in fact, where this is happening. Right on the front porch.

"Are you scared?"

I breathe out a laugh. "I'm not scared of anything."

She drops to her knees and I look around the property in front of me, just for added measure. Just what we came here for —solitude.

As soon as her mouth wraps around my head, all modesty and care diminishes. Suddenly, we could have an audience and I wouldn't give a shit.

My head drops back, fingers tangling in her hair. Mouth agape and cock twitching in delight. She peers up at me with her big, green wistful eyes. Watching me watch her, she drags her tongue from my head down to my shaft, then sweeps underneath before sucking one of my balls into her mouth. "Holy shit, babe."

I can feel her mouth smile around my cock. And it hits me that she's never sucked my dick before. How did she learn how to do this so good? Who else has she been with? My heartbeat picks up and I find myself replaying the last two years and thinking about who I may have seen her with. No one. I've never seen her with any guys. Could this be her first time giving head?

"You're so good at this. How'd you learn?" Sounded better in my head, but the words just spit out.

She takes me out of her mouth, wipes her hand across her mouth and says, "Learning as I go."

I breathe out a sigh of relief. We might all have a past, but I just can't imagine Vi ever being with anyone else.

Picking up her pace, she sucks harder and deeper. My head hitting her tonsils, then coming back out for air. Another long sweep of her tongue down my length and she begins stroking as she sucks. My chest rises and falls as I breathe in shallow breaths.

"Fuck," I mutter as my fist clenches around her hair, guiding my cock in and out of her mouth. My hips rock back and forth as I bite down on my lip. "I'm gonna come," I forewarn her. She doesn't stop, just keeps sucking on me like my cock is the best thing she's ever tasted. One final thrust and I'm back in her throat, shooting down the back of it. Tension releases, electricity shooting through my body. My heart rate slows down and my fingers untangle from her black locks.

"That was fucking amazing," I tell her. "Now, it's time to return the favor."

Her fingers run the rim of her lips and she smirks. "What did you have in mind?"

I don't answer with words; instead, I kick off my jeans that were lingering around my ankles, pull my shirt off and toss it off the porch, then drop down in front of her where she's still on her knees. "Lie down," I demand. When she does, I jerk her shorts off in one swift pull, not even unzipping them first.

Sweeping her panties to the side with one hand, I take in the view of her dripping, tight pussy. I trail a finger between her lips, look at her, then suck it into my mouth. "You're dripping, baby." Her cheeks tinge pink and the shyness about her turns me on. Pulling my finger out slowly after lathering it up, I slide it inside of her, watching her eyes—searching for that look that tells me I'm right where she wants me.

I move in and out of her, adding another finger. Curling the tips and vibrating them against her G-spot. She lets out a subtle moan that tells me to keep doing what I'm doing. "You like that?"

She responds with a nod, then arches her back off the boards of the porch. As soon as she starts getting into it, I pull my fingers out.

"What are you doing?" She pouts, wanting more of what I'm giving her.

"Making it worth your while." I slide her damp panties all the way off and drop them to the side. My naked body glides up hers until my mouth finds her lips. I suck her lip ring in between my teeth and devour her entire mouth. Taking her tongue hostage and grinding my cock against her, feeling like I could go for round two already.

I break the kiss, then come back up, pulling her with me. With a hand behind her back, I unclasp her bra. She pulls it off all the way and gets rid of it. I slide down, stopping at her perky breasts and sucking her nipple in my mouth.

Then I keep going until my face is level with her pussy. With two fingers, I pad at her clit, then sweep my tongue up from her asshole to her entrance. My tongue darts inside of her continuously as I keep rubbing her sensitive nub. Her hips buck, her fingers now in my hair as she rides my face.

"Oh my God, Zed. Ugghh, don't stop."

Didn't plan on it.

I slide two fingers inside of her, still teasing her clit. Going knuckle-deep, I drum at the spot that sends her into a moaning frenzy.

She places a hand on her breast and begins kneading at her own skin. Her mouth gaping and her eyes full of lust and desire.

Her entire body shudders and I watch her eyes as she comes

undone. The sounds that escape her have me wanting to be inside of her, sharing this orgasm with her.

Before she comes down, I pull my fingers out and ram my cock into her pussy. Grabbing her legs and letting them cradle over my forearms, I spread them wide open.

I thrust so deep that her body scoots across the porch, but she continues to cry out in a pleasurable moan. Harder and faster, I feel her walls clench around me. I bite down, hard, grinding my teeth and feeling her release drip down my cock. I don't stop. I keep going until I'm on the brink of explosion. Then, I pull out, flip her over on her knees and go right back inside.

My fingers cling to her hips, my nails bedding into her skin without piercing it. Even as the skin on my knees begins to peel from the burn against the wood of the porch, I keep going. My pelvic bone crashes against her ass and she continues to cry out, almost screaming.

Electricity zaps at my insides for the second time tonight, filling me with this insatiable need to combust. I surge inside of her nimbly. Relishing in the wet, sticky, warmth that envelops my cock. She feels like heaven. An angel in my hell. I thrust again and again, writhing in pleasure until I explode deep inside of her.

My cock twitches as I pull out. Somehow we've managed to move about three feet from where we started. Vi turns around, drops to her ass, and lets out a heavy breath. "Holy shit." She wipes a hand across her forehead, sweeping away the sweat that's pooled at her hairline.

I drop down beside her. My back pressed to the porch and one leg bent up. My cock flops around on my thigh, jerking like a dead fish as I come down from the high.

Vi lies on her side, propping her head up with her hand and puts the other over my chest.

"Welcome home," I say through a ragged breath. My eyes close, but her lips make their way to mine. A soft, subtle kiss that's so much more than anything sex can give me.

I'm not sure how I got this lucky. Only weeks ago, I was ready to die. But Vi finding me that day was the best thing that's ever happened to me.

I open my eyes and find her right in front of me, wearing a cheesy-ass smile. "Hey," I say to her.

"Hey." She kisses me again, and again, and again.

We lie there for a good twenty minutes in perfect silence before I realize we should probably find a way inside this house or drive back to Redwood for the keys.

Once we're dressed, I go to my truck to get my phone so I can call the inn and have Mrs. Mayberry check my room for the house keys.

And wouldn't you fucking know it, the keys are sitting right next to my phone in the cupholder.

"Hey, Vi," I call out to her as she stands on the porch.

She looks my way and sees me dangling the keys in the air. Her palm meets her forehead and she laughs.

I jog up to her, hand her the keys, and let her do the honors of unlocking the door. "Guess we screwed on the porch for nothing," I say to her.

"I actually liked it. Wouldn't mind doing it again later." She winks.

We walk in, I take a deep breath, wrap my arm around Vi's waist, and take a look at my new home. It's so surreal that I have everything in my life that I never knew I wanted. If this is a dream, I never want to wake up. I've been beaten down, stomped on, got up and stomped on a few people myself, but I'm alive, and for the first time in my life, I'm ready to live

I got the girl next door. I might not like people, but I sure as fuck love her.

CHAPTER TWENTY-SEVEN

ZED

Two Months Later

The entire gym is packed and I feel like everyone I know is looking at me, wondering why I'm not in a cap and gown. Then again, if they know me, they're probably not surprised at all. I've always been a joke to everyone in this town.

I'm the kid who lost his mom, had a fuck-up for a father, and raised hell because I got away with it. At least, that's how I'm looked at.

Who am I really? I'm a guy who had a rough past, a missing soul, and a wounded heart. I fed myself off the pain of others, smiled at their sadness, and had an ego ten times too big for my head.

Who am I now? The same guy.

I haven't changed—much.

Now, I don't live just for myself; I live for my girl. She's the reason my heart still ticks, even if it is still black as coal—she loves it and me anyway.

I might have changed in some aspects. I'm a little more mature, but still young. I don't push people around, but I certainly don't let people knock me down. Most importantly, I want to live and not die—not yet, anyway.

For the most part, I'm still the same guy I've always been. I'll still fight to the death for the ones I love. Got my boys by my side, and on the weekends, a beer in my hand.

I don't live in the past anymore, but it's made me who I am. For so long I wanted to forget, now I hope I never do. It's a reminder of where these scars came from and how I overcame everything life threw at me.

They might call me a sadistic reaper, but I call myself a fucking warrior.

And this girl sitting next to me, she's a damn saint.

She puts up with my shit, loves me hard, and lets me love her back.

My fellow classmates all come down, looking sharp as hell in their cap and gowns. Marni is walking with Talon. Wyatt with Tommy. Willa with Lars.

Vi nudges my shoulder. "I really wish you were up there. You deserve to be."

"Nah, I really don't. I never put any effort into school." Maybe it's because I always knew that I'd never use the diploma. Not that I don't plan to work because I do. I might have a shitload of money, but I'm not a complete loser. I'm just not sure what I want to do yet.

I give Vi's thigh a squeeze and look over at her. "You plan on walking in graduation next year?" Vi does her school work virtually, but she'll still have the option to walk. I hope she does. It might be a mundane thing to most, but if I had one regret in life, this might be it. Not walking with my boys. The guys I've been friends with since grade school.

"I think I will. You gonna be here to watch me?"

With a snarl, I side-eye her. "You fucking kidding me? I'll be front and center. I'm your biggest fan, baby." I throw an arm around her shoulder and pull her close. Her head rests on my chest and it's as if my entire body was sculpted to fit her perfectly.

Principal Burton takes the stage and begins calling off names. Redwood isn't big, but it's not really that small either. We've got about one hundred and sixty people in our class and I'm already bored as fuck.

We finally get through the *B*'s.

"Thomas Chambers," Principal Burton calls out.

Tommy walks up in his purple gown and white Converse that say 'Class of Fucking 2020' on one and 'Farewell High School' on the other in black marker. It's just like him.

I let out my deafening whistle and clap my hands, grabbing the attention of my neighbors.

Forty-five minutes later, we make it to the *M*'s. Wyatt goes up and accepts his diploma. Few minutes later, Willa's name is called. Now there's a girl who *deserves* this. Next to Vi, Willa is one of the strongest and bravest girls I know.

It's crazy how something so dark and tragic can bond us.

Willa takes her diploma, shakes Principal Burton's hand, and then I'm not sure what the hell she does next.

"What is she doing?" I whisper to Vi.

"No idea."

She's just standing there on stage with her mouth in the shape of an O. Principal Burton is calling someone over while Willa waddles over to the end of the stage. Lars hurries to her side, claps a hand over his mouth, and holy shit, I think her water just broke.

Someone comes on the stage with a mop and begins cleaning it up.

I can't help but laugh because it's a great fucking ending to this chapter of our lives.

"Come on," Vi says, pulling me up.

We maneuver through the crowd on the bleachers and head straight for the doors and out the gym, where Lars is leading

Willa.

"What the hell was that?" I ask him.

"Her water broke. It's baby time, baby." Lars beams with excitement.

"Ahhh, it's so wet," Willa frowns. "And...oh, God. Another one." She curls over, holding her stomach. "Vi, can you come to the bathroom with me?"

"Yeah, of course," Vi says, then looks at me and walks away.

"Dude," I draw out. "Are you ready for this shit? You're about to be a dad."

Lars runs his fingers through his hair and takes in a deep breath. "Ready or not."

"Come on, maybe you should sit down. You look pale." I lead Lars over to a bench in the empty student center. He drops down, legs spread, and leans forward. "What if I fuck this kid up?"

"Impossible."

"No. No, it's very possible. I mean, look at us. We're all just kids ourselves. How the hell am I gonna raise a daughter? She's not even here and I already wanna hold onto her forever just so I can protect her."

"That's how I know it's impossible for you to fuck up. You're probably the only one out of all four of us who is incapable of fucking this up."

Vi and Willa come out of the bathroom and Willa doesn't look too hot.

"We need to go." Willa waddles over with her legs stretched apart.

Lars and I get up and meet them halfway. I look at Vi who seems concerned, then to Willa. "Well, on the bright side, that gown covers your piss stain."

Vi bumps her shoulder to mine and scoffs. "Zed!"

At least Lars and Willa find it funny.

"So, you heading to the hospital?" I ask.

Willa breathes through a contraction, grabbing Lars' arm and

squeezing it so tight that I'm not sure who's in more pain here—
her or him. We all just watch her silently, and I'm not sure about
them, but I'm so glad it's her and not me because that shit looks
painful as hell. I don't think I'll ever be able to knock Vi up for
that reason alone. I'd lose my mind trying to figure out how I
could take her pain away.

A group of girls walk by, gawking for far too long. I'm really
biting my tongue here, but the constant staring is really starting
to piss me off.

"Do you all have a problem? Haven't you ever seen a pregnant
girl in labor before?" Vi hisses, taking matters into her own
hands. That's my fucking girl.

The girls all snap their eyes back in front of them and keep
walking without a word.

Once the contraction passes, Willa's a brand-new person. She
looks at Lars, who's rubbing his arm in agony. "I need to go home
and take a shower first, then I think we should go in."

Lars takes Willa by the hand, gives us a wave, and they're off.

In the gym, everyone starts hooting and hollering. There's
clapping and whistling, then everyone in the graduating class
shouts, "Class of twenty-twenty!"

"Glad it's them and not us," I whisper to Vi.

"No kidding. I'm almost positive I never want kids."

"Glad we're on the same page there."

∞

"HOW LONG DOES THIS SHIT TAKE?" I slouch down further into my
chair in the waiting room.

"It could take hours," Marni says from across the room.

Talon pipes up, leans forward, and presses his elbows to his
knees. "I've heard it can take days. Those things don't come out
until they're ready."

"Days?" I huff. "No way. Once that water shit comes out, the baby has to come. It's like a little fish in there. Can't breathe without it." I sure hope it doesn't take hours. All I want to do is go back home and crawl into bed with Vi for the rest of the summer. Although, we're all crashing at Talon's tonight. He was supposed to be throwing this raging graduation night party, but that's all changed. Canceled it at the last minute and here we are.

All bullshit aside, this is what we do for each other. One of us falls down, we help each other up. A body needs to be taken care of, we take care of that fucking body. Revenges come to life, demons are buried, and we shine a light on each other that only we can see.

I'll be here for the birth of every one of their kids. Hopefully the next one won't be for a very long time, but one day. Lucky for them, they'll never have to do the same because I'm not having kids. I'm too selfish for that shit.

The waiting room door opens and we all jump up. As soon as we realize it's Tommy, we all sit back down.

"Dude, where the hell do you put all that?" I ask as he walks in with an armful of snacks.

"This could take hours. Maybe even days. A man's gotta eat."

"See," Talon points with a serious tone, "told you it could take days."

I brush him off with a sweep of my hand. "That's not true at all. It's a scientific fact that—"

I'm cut off when the doors open again. We all jump back up, and this time, it's Lars. He's wearing some blue paper outfit that makes him look like a very smart, yet very rebellious and young doctor. He pulls off his cute little hair net and throws it in the air like it's the grad cap he didn't get to throw. "We got a baby girl!"

Side by side, we walk the halls of the hospital. Seems like just yesterday we were walking the halls of Redwood High. We're going to meet the first little offspring of the bunch. The second girl to steal Lars' heart.

I hesitate at the doorway, still feeling a bit out of place after everything that went down.

Everyone huddles around Willa and the baby, congratulating and hugging her while I stand back and observe. I give my best affection and congratulations from afar. Vi stands beside me, still not quite on that level with this group.

"What are you guys doing? Get in here," Marni says, calling us over.

It's crazy. All of it. How someone can go from being a stranger, to an enemy, to a friend, to being family. That's what we are. We're all family.

With Vi's hand in mine, we join them. I'm not sure what it is that comes over me next. But as soon as I lay eyes on that baby girl, I realize the entire world is screwed. She's got Lars as a dad and me and the guys as her uncles; no guy in existence stands a chance.

She's beautiful. Perfect, really.

Suddenly, everything makes sense. Everything that did happen, and everything that didn't. It all brought us to this moment.

It's been a hell of a ride, but we came out on top.

From start to finish. And everything in between.

ZED

One Year Later

Vi comes walking out of the bathroom, looking hot as hell in a black sundress. Her hair is piled on top of her head in a messy bun, skull earrings hang from her lobes, and she's sporting a pair of black Chucks. As I've said many times, she's my kind of sexy.

Her forehead wrinkles as she looks down at her dress and then up at me. "Too much?"

I prop my elbow on the counter and scan her entire body from head to toe as I bite hard at the corner of my lip. "Fuck no. I just can't wait to peel that dress off of you." My cock twitches at the same time as my phone begins vibrating on the counter. "It's Lars," I tell her, ignoring the call.

"Yeah. We're late. We better get going." Her feet move toward the door, but I eat up the space between us.

"Ten minutes? That's all I need." I grab her by the waist, pull her close, and draw in a deep breath of her sweet skin. My lips trail her collarbone and it's taking everything in me not to devour her right here and now.

An audible breath escapes her as she tilts her head to the side. Goosebumps shimmy down her arm while her nipples harden against the fabric of her dress. "Babe, we've gotta go." She draws back, looks in my eyes, and licks her lips—she's fucking killing me. "But, I promise as soon as we get home, my body will be yours to do whatever you want with."

Her lips press to mine and I let out a low growl. "Mmm," I hum, "Is that a promise?"

Her mouth ghosts mine, sharing my breaths. "We could make it a dare instead. I dare you to make me scream so loud that the pictures on the walls rattle."

Sliding my hand up her dress, I cup her crotch. Her damp panties telling me all I need to know. "You know I never back down from a challenge."

"Exactly why I'm challenging you."

I push her panties to the side and slide a finger up her slit. She lets out a subtle moan. "Well, I've got a little wager of my own." I push a finger inside her. "I make you scream now, and later we scream together."

Another finger slides in. Her arousal coating my knuckles. She's so wet and I know that she's not stopping me now. "Fine."

"Fine?" I take a few steps as we stay connected like a puzzle. "That's all you have to say?" She drops down on the couch with parted legs and I crouch in front of her. Her bare pussy looks back at me, dripping with desire.

As her head drops back, her mouth gapes. "Show me what you got, Rebel."

My fingers pump continuously as I dart my tongue out and lick her clit with enough pressure to cause her body to jolt.

Her panties get in the way, so I move my hand and slide them down until they are dangling around one ankle above her shoes. I return to fingering her and flicking my tongue at her sensitive nub.

When she grabs a fistful of my hair, she pushes down and

arches her back. My fingers thrust harder and faster, hitting her G-spot while she lets out a whimper. "Fuck me, Zed."

"Oh no, a deal's a deal," I say between licks of her sweet pussy.

Fingers tangle in my hair, and she tugs before losing all control. "Oh God," she cries out. "Uggh, baby. I'm coming."

As soon as I suck her clit between my teeth, I feel her walls clench around my fingers and her arousal spills onto my hand. I keep going, riding out her orgasm until she relaxes.

"Fuck the deal." I stand up, drop my pants to my ankles and grab her waist to flip her over on her knees. In two seconds flat, my dick is inside of her. It doesn't take long. I pump a few times while grazing my thumb over her asshole. My body fills up with combustion. A few more thrusts into her tight, warm pussy and I release inside of her.

My movements stop and I pull out slowly. With a turned head, she looks back at me. "Round two when we get home. Right now, I need to get cleaned up because we are so late."

I give her a wink before helping her up. She goes to walk away, but I grab her wrist and pull her back to me. My lips press to hers. "I love you."

She smiles against my mouth. "I love you more."

∞

"Happy birthday to you. Happy birthday to you. Happy birthday, dear Alessi. Happy birthday to you."

"Blow. Blow 'em out," Lars says as he holds Alessi over the cake. She doesn't blow. Doesn't even try. Instead, she stretches a hand down and grabs a fistful of pink frosting with a look on her face that says, 'I do what I want.'

Everyone busts out laughing, including me. It is pretty fucking cute.

Willa takes Alessi from Lars and he joins me, Tommy, and Talon on the other side of the six-foot table in Lars' back yard.

There's pink everywhere. Pink balloons, pink ribbons, pink paper things hanging from the trees. Guess that's what you get when you have a girl. Way too much pink.

Vi is helping Marni with cutting the cake, and Willa is now chasing after Alessi who has smeared pink frosting all over her dress.

Lars digs into a cooler and starts passing out beers. I take one from him, flip the top to crack it open, and take a long swig. "Raging party, man. Though you look like you're ready to cash out." I look at the invisible watch on my wrist. "It's only what, two in the afternoon?" I tease.

"Yeah." He stretches his arms up with a yawn. "You know how we roll now. Bedtime at nine, naps at noon, and a two-beer limit."

"Speaking of, how's school going?" Talon asks. I'm not sure if he's talking to me or the other guys.

"You." He points at me. "I'm talking to you."

"Oh. Just finished that shit. I'm officially a high school graduate." A whole summer of classes and half of a fall semester and I was able to finish. Probably won't ever need the diploma, but I did it, nonetheless.

"So what's next? College? Full-time job?" Lars asks before taking a swig of his beer.

"No fucking clue," I tell them. "What about you guys?"

I know that Lars is taking classes at a community college in the city, along with Marni. Wyatt and Tommy are at UCLA but home for the weekend. Talon is sort of at a stalemate, much like me.

Tommy looks down at his foot as he taps his toe to the ground. "I honestly don't have a clue what I'm doing after college. Art is really all I'm passionate about."

Lars finishes off his beer and tosses his can in the garbage in front of us. "I've got the business degree coming, but no plans after my four years are up."

"So, here you guys are, all going to college and you don't even know why." I laugh. "That's exactly why I'm not going."

Everyone always drills it in your head that you graduate and you go to college. But what they don't tell you is that college isn't for everyone. Sure, we've all got money to live on as it is, but even if I didn't, I'd probably do something like trade school to be a mechanic or try and start up my own business.

I snap my fingers, feeling like I might be on to something. "Guys," I spit out. "What if we say fuck what everyone wants us to do and we do something for ourselves. For our futures. For our kids." *Not that I plan on having any, but it flowed well.*

"I'm listening," Talon says, taking a plate of cake from Marni as she passes them out.

Marni lends an ear and listens in while she holds out another plate to Tommy. He shakes his head, turning the cake down.

"Let's start something of our own."

Tommy quirks a brow. "As in, business partners?" The idea must excite him because he changes his mind and takes the plate from Marni. He takes a big bite and talks through the chew. "Go on."

"Yeah. Tommy has the design abilities. Lars has the business skills. I'm pretty good at negotiations. And Talon, well…he's a man of many trades."

"I think it's a great idea," Marni says, offering her two cents.

Vi comes out of nowhere with two plates of cake. "What's a great idea?" she asks Marni.

"The guys were talking about starting up a business together."

Vi looks at me and chuckles as I stand here now double-fisting two beers. "Like what? A brewery?"

A low growl climbs up my throat at the sight of her. She looks so fucking sexy in her black little sundress, even with that sarcastic mouth. "No. Not a brewery." I set my beers down on the grill and grab her by the waist, pulling her over to me. She stands in front of me, my arms wrapped around her waist. "We're not sure yet. Just toying with the idea."

Talon grabs one of the unopened beers off the grill and examines the can. "Actually, that's not a bad idea. We're not at the legal drinking age, yet. But it's definitely something we can start working at. I think a brewery is a badass idea."

Lars runs with the idea. "We could get a warehouse, a distribution center, maybe even open a local pub with our own beer on tap. Hell, we could even use local crops."

"I could do the marketing and design aspect," Tommy says.

The more we talk about it, the more exciting it sounds. A brewery run by four childhood friends. "Rebel Bros. Brewery," I spit out, liking the ring to it.

Talon nods in agreement. "I like it."

I slap a hand to Tommy's shoulder. "Sounds like we've got a new adventure to embark on."

Lars holds out his fist. "Let's do this."

Talon bumps it back. "From start to finish."

Tommy joins in.

Lastly, I bump my knuckles to theirs. "And everything in between."

The End.

WANT MORE? Read the bonus short story NOW! See how the Rebels are doing 10 years later!
GET IT HERE!
or go to http://bit.ly/redwoodrebelsbonus

SPEAK UP

If you or someone you know is struggling emotionally, or has concerns about their mental health, there are ways to get help.

You don't have to struggle in silence.

Call 1-800-273-TALK

ALSO BY RACHEL LEIGH

Redwood Rebels Series

Book One: Striker

Book Two: Heathen

Book Three: Vandal

Book Four: Reaper

Redwood High Series

(All books can be read as a stand-alone)

Book One: Like Gravity

Book Two: Like You

Book Three: Like Hate

Duet

Chasing You

Catching You

Standalones:

Guarded

Four

Find me on Facebook @rachelleighauthor

Reader's Group: Rachel's Ramblers

FROM THE AUTHOR

Thank you so much for taking the time to read Reaper. I hope you've enjoyed the series! It's bittersweet that it's over, but I'm glad I was able to give these boy's their HEAs.

Bloggers and Bookstagramers, THANK YOU for all you do!

A big thank you to Greys Promotions for all your amazing work with promoting Reaper. You are all so wonderful to work with.

Thank you to Rebecca, Fairest Reviews and Editing Service, for another amazing edit and for being so flexible with me. It's always a pleasure working with you. And, thank you to Rumi Kahn for proofreading!

Thank you to the best PA in the world, Carolina Leon, for everything you do day in and day out. Love you!

Thank you to Lori for driving to TN roundtrip so I could use the time to write Reaper. You're such an amazing friend!

Sara Cate, thank you for helping me make decisions and for being such a good friend.

Rebel Readers Street Team, I love you all so much, and I appreciate all your help getting the word out about my books!

My readers group, Rachel's Ramblers, thank you for being a part of my happy place.

Thank you to Kate at Ya'll. That Graphic for making me all these gorgeous covers and teasers.

As well as Ashes and Vellicor for the amazing graphics!

A HUGE shoutout to my alpha and beta readers, Amanda, Aurora, Rachel, Christine, Kerri, Krystal, and Nikki! Thank you for reading and helping me polish up Reaper. I appreciate you all so much.

I can't wait to create more worlds and bring more characters to life. I have some exciting things planned. If you'd like to stay up to date on what's to come, join my readers group, Rachel's Ramblers. I'd love to have you.

ABOUT THE AUTHOR

Rachel Leigh writes Contemporary and New Adult Romance with twists and turns, suspense and steam. She resides in West Michigan with her husband, three kids, and a couple fur babies.

Rachel lives in leggings, overuses emojis, and survives on books and coffee. Writing is her passion. Her goal is to take readers on an adventure with her words, while showing them that even on the darkest days, love conquers all.

f facebook.com/rachelleighauthor

© instagram.com/rachelleighauthor

BB bookbub.com/profile/rachel-leigh

g goodreads.com/rachelleigh

a amazon.com/author/rachelleighauthor

CPSIA information can be obtained
at www.ICGtesting.com
Printed in the USA
LVHW090357270723
753091LV00007B/585

9 781088 145470